THE WEIRD
and whatnot

July 5, 2019

The Weird and Whatnot Issue No. 2 (July 2019)
© 2019 the Weird and Whatnot, LLC.

THE EDITING TEAM

Valerie Haskin
Faralee Pozo
Joshua Wilkins

TECHNICAL DIRECTOR

Lance Whitaker

ART DIRECTOR

Scott Grove

READERS & VOLUNTEERS

Kimberly Wallace, Emily Leggett, Arlene Erickson, Suzanne Chappell, Hannah Azure, Boydell Bown, Anne Bown, Acell Bown, Fae Whitaker, Tyler Watson

Interior Illustrations by Scott Grove

Cover art by L.A. Spooner

The Weird and Whatnot is an ever-growing community of authors, artists, poets, and readers. If you would like to be a part of our Weird community, come to theweirdandwhatnot.com and pull up a chair. We publish quarterly in both print and e-book, with featured stories and book reviews on our website. Our call for submissions is always open and free.

Note from the Editor

As I thought about my feelings on this issue and The Weird and Whatnot, I could only really think about one thing. That feeling is how lucky I am to be a part of this project, and this community. As I sat in gatherings or editing meetings, I would look around at the people around me and barely hold back a smile. I had friends who came to meetings as volunteers who I didn't think would last an hour and ended up staying well into the night, laughing and working with us. Something about a good story transcends our ability to describe it. We can feel it in our souls and underneath the sentences and words there is a meaning that reaches deeper.

Basically, what I'm trying to say with all of that rambling is that stories have always meant more to me than I can say, and that to be a part of this group of people who feel the same is one of the greatest blessings of my life. It is as simple as that. I'm lucky to be able to bring these wonderful stories to a wider audience, and I'm lucky to be surrounded by wonderful people who want to do the same.I can confidently say that each one of these stories has impacted us, and that is why we want to bring them to you. We want you to be a part of the family.

This issue was made through a hailstorm of laughs, hard work, set backs, and an absolute passion for what we were doing. I hope that as you read through this second issue of The Weird and Whatnot that you will feel the love that we have for these stories. Each one is a phenomenal tale that we are ecstatic to present to you. Let's get weird everyone!

Joshua Wilkins

The Editing Team

Contents

—

SLEEPOVER BY LUKE SPOONER

Luke Spooner is an artist and illustator living in the South of England. Having attained First Class degree in illustration from the University of Portsmouth his current projects and commissions now include illustrations and covers for books, magazines, graphic novels, books aimed at children, conceptual design and business branding. Find more information about him and his work at www.carrionhouse.com

SLEEPOVER AT GRANDMA'S

GARY BULLER

A CLOCK FACE is hammered into the wall, high above the bed. The roman numerals are higgledy-piggledy, and the hands bent outwards, like the whiskers of a cat. There aren't any cogs or mechanisms behind it, only floral wallpaper, but it keeps time just the same. You can't take your eyes off it. Grandma owns many unusual things, but this must be the weirdest. The old woman said she hammered the components in place herself. You smiled agreeably because Grandma frightens you sometimes.

Marnie clings to your back even though it is very stuffy beneath the duvet. Her pajamas are damp with perspiration, and her skin is slick where it touches yours. Her breath tickles the nape of your neck, but you daren't move. Children are to be seen and not heard, especially at bedtime, Grandma said.

Your feet are prickly and hot within their woolen bed socks. Marnie told you to remove them before you both climbed into bed, but you were distracted by the strange sounds coming from the attic space.

You regret not paying attention to Marnie now.

Grandma told you and Marnie not to mention these sounds to your parents and that if you did, they wouldn't believe you anyway. You thought this might be true. Grandma bakes cakes and knits scarves, occasionally she makes Sunday lunch for the family, but sometimes she acts differently when mum and dad aren't around.

Silence fills the room like cotton wool, the only sounds coming from the television downstairs, and you begin to doubt your own ears.

"I hope she goes to bed soon." You feel as much as hear Marnie's tremulous whisper caress your hair. "Then we can throw off the sheets?"

The mumble of the television stops suddenly. Grandma's walking stick thuds rhythmically to the alcove at the bottom of the stairs. Her voice rises to find you. It is sharp and scratchy like rusty barbed wire.

"Don't think I can't hear you," she says, snatching a raspy breath. "I might be old but there's nothing wrong with my ears." Moonlight pours through a crack in the curtains and draws a line up the wall. The minute hand of the clock shivers with trepidation. Grandma waits. You sense her down there, a statue in the darkness. Marnie is aware of this too, you can tell by the way she holds her breath. Her lips part but she closes them again, somehow you know it's an apology.

After a prolonged silence, Grandma returns to the living room and the comfy chair sighs under her weight. The television comes to life again, and the minute hand of the clock takes an unsteady step forward. Thoughts of your parents occupy your mind. Dad making you laugh with his silly stories as Marnie (too old for this) rolls her eyes. Mum taking you and Marnie to the reservoir and picking wimberries on the grassy embankment. Mum and dad were so excited at the prospect of their date night, but strangely reluctant to let you sleep at Grandma's for the first time. You didn't like the way mum's eyes lingered from the passenger side window as you waved goodbye from Grandma's front step.

You all but forget the lumps and bumps of the mattress which make home between your ribs, waiting for sleep like a passenger at a rural train station. You watch the clock.

The cramp begins as an acorn sized knot in your side, below the spot where Marnie's hand rests. Its painful embrace has woken you numerous times before, more often than not in your calves. No amount of sucking through teeth or rubbing seems to alleviate them. Mum said the pains were caused by dehydration and insisted on plenty of water before bed, but it doesn't always work. Your weighty lids spring open as the pain spreads like a bruise across your side. The muscles grow taught. This is bad.

Marnie must have fallen asleep, because she jerks a little before lifting her hand. You inhale and exhale through your nostrils, bite down on your lip, try to stay still but it's no good.

"Don't," Marnie breathes.

The duvet is heavy and rustles like it's filled with a thousand plastic bags. You take a corner and peel it away. Night air cools the droplets of sweat which have formed on your skin but agitates the muscles, which contract further. Your teeth burrow deeper into your bottom lip, drawing blood, and a tear caresses your cheek. You squeeze Marnie's hand. Her grip suddenly tightens, and you sense her look to the ceiling.

Something has awakened in the attic. It is the thing which makes strange sounds, like sheets dragging across floorboards. Your stomach fills with ice-water, and the cramp goes into overdrive. Arching your back instinctively, you release Marnie's hand and knead the spot as quietly as possible. One of the mattress springs which has made home between your ribs frees. Compressed for hours, it trembles before suddenly expanding with a loud twang.

The television falls silent.

"I'm not going to tell you twice," Grandma screeches, but she is the least of your worries. The thing upstairs quickens pace, towards the exit, towards the spindle stairs leading to the landing outside. Marnie begins to cry. You feel her shoulders shaking and hear her faint gasps for breath. This unnerves you because she is usually very strong, even standing up to the bullies at school when they pick on you.

The spindle stairs groan as something descends, one step at a time. The minute hand of the clock trembles and moves backward from twenty past ten to quarter to nine. The air cools further. You sit upright, but it's like moving in treacle, like the world is spinning a little slower. Marnie's face is unusually pallid, but her cheeks are rosy. Clouds spill from her open mouth. She looks to you and then the slide door. Not one, but two shapes appear behind the frosted glass and the door rolls gradually open.

They make a sound like October leaves as they ghost into the room, a funeral procession in black. Their heads are bowed beneath narrow robes. Hands like arthritic branches stretch out before them, tasting the air with the tips of their fingers. For a surreal moment it looks like they move underwater, something about the way the folds of material undulate like seaweed. You glance briefly to the clock, and the hands vibrate furiously in place.

Marnie whimpers.

They smell like dust and pennies. You know they are old, much older than grandma and perhaps older than the house itself. It is an instinctive knowing, like a mouse recognizing a hawk when the shadow descends. In another universe, outside this torpid lacuna, Grandma's cane goes thud, thud, thud.

It is only when Marnie grabs your upper arm that you find yourself standing atop the mattress. Fear is fertile soil and courage has germinated someplace deep inside, born out of necessity. Wiggling from her grasp, you pad across the uneven surface and extend a hand.

The creature shrinks back and emits an avian screech as the hood of its robe bobs and weaves. It turns to its companion and this is when you grasp its robe between finger and thumb. The cold material feels papery and thin, like a bat's wing. You pull with all your might, as quickly as the turgid air will allow, and the creature turns inside out, an umbrella in a gale.

The ghastly sheet flails and resists, desperately attempting to rectify itself, but there is a strange weightlessness to it. Angry screams vibrate through your bones as your arm is dragged this way and that, but you stand firm.

The second creature looms close and the coppery smell of pennies intensifies. It moves in slow motion, navigating around the bed like creeping death. Marnie's pale hand cuts through the darkness, grips its robe and whips back. You turn to find her standing at your side, equal parts fear and grim determination on her face, as whatever-it-is resists. Your teeth chatter and vibrate as their screams make home inside your head, bleaching your vision white. Your fingers grow numb from their constant battle, and you feel the creature slipping away. Finally, it jerks free and flies in circles around the room. You catch a glimpse of black eyes and mean, little teeth.

The door almost bursts off its hinges. Grandma hobbles into the room, all round and wrinkled like a vegetable left in the sun. A shawl hangs over her shoulders, and her hair is lank and gray. Moonlight reflects in her spectacles, and her mouth is a flat line.

"Enough," she says.

Raising her stick, Grandma points to the clock on the wall and the creatures freeze mid-air. Marnie releases the one she was holding, and it remains stationary before her like a frozen shroud on a washing line.

"I told you to be quiet," Grandma scolds you both. The hand which holds the walking-stick is trembling. "I said no noise. Do you think that was for my benefit? Well, do you?" Her stern gaze travels from you to Marnie and back again. "If your parents hadn't . . ." she takes a deep breath. "Well, anyway. Let's tidy this mess up." The handle of her walking stick is a brass goat head. It is tarnished, and one of the sapphire eyes is missing. Mum told you the stick was passed from mother to daughter all the way back to the seventeen hundreds. She said one day it might be yours.

Grandma gestures with the stick again and the clock turns backward, slowly at first but building up speed. The creatures move in reverse, hopelessly recounting the steps they've already taken until they skulk back through the sliding door. Grandma steps out of their way, her spine against the wall, and watches them shuffle down the passage and up the spiral staircase. Soon they are back in the attic. You hear them slink along the floor like rotten silk before falling silent.

The hands of the clock stop abruptly, glowing red. No one speaks for a moment.

"Right, bedtime," Grandma says, finally. "You're both going to be tired in the morning."

She approaches, and you and Marnie climb under the duvet. You remove the woolen socks and toss them to the floor. Grandma tucks you in.

"What were they, Grandma?" Marnie asks, and the old woman recoils a little. Her thumb rubs the snout of the brass goat, and she slowly exhales.

"I guess you could say they came with the house," she says.

Her lips feel itchy as she plants them on your forehead. She smells of powdery, floral perfume. Her eyes don't leave yours as she straightens up, and in that moment, Grandma almost looks like somebody else.

"Sleep." She says as she leaves, but sleep is a stranger. You stare at the clock and listen to Marnie breathe. It sounds like she has finally drifted off, but something bothers you, a mental splinter digging just under the skin of your consciousness. As time passes you start to wonder if it was actually all a dream, a strange nightmare conjured up by less familiar surroundings. At that moment something captures your attention. A copper spring protrudes from the center of the clock face where the two hands join. It is small and wiry and bobs up and down—a small cog balances on the end of it. The hands themselves are even more crooked than before and the wallpaper behind them is singed.

You watch closely, willing the minute hand to proceed with every ounce of your being, but nothing happens.

Marnie murmurs and turns over. The mattress groans.

Upstairs, something shuffles along the floor.

Gary Buller is an author from Manchester England where he lives with his partner Lisa and daughters Holly and Evie. He grew up in the Peak District where the hauntingly beautiful landscapes inspired him to write. He is a huge fan of all things macabre, and loves a tale with a twist. He is a member of the Horror Writers Association.

JOHN GREY

STEVENS OVERDOSED, I'VE BEEN ALONE SINCE

In the chill of deep two-moon night,
warm is the only form of consciousness.
From lab to faux-home Quonset hut,
I shudder the path of least resistance.

I have my orders and they're chilly enough.
Pound the rocks into chemical submission.
Isolate quarks in mesons.
Measure the radiation.
And, while you're at it,
the space-time relationships of the universe.
Gauge the gravity.
Lock onto the air.
Study plasmas and weather,
photon energy and wave-particle duality.
And remember, you're second to no one
in your knowledge of quantum mechanics.
When you're done with all that,
poke and prod the man.

That is ongoing and let it be on record
that this living is just death in another guise.
My blood runs cold even when
the radium burners run hot.

The corpse is done for the day.

I've learned one thing in my ten years here:

space is a billion lifetimes of unknowable truths,

as viewed from the stones of a graveyard.

The lilies wilt by my bed in sympathy.

I'm oblivious to the winter lights outside.

Besides, I'm soured on beauty,

And memory also.

I've invited every other place I've ever lived

to this intergalactic backwater.

but no place will come.

Houston told me to think of myself as a lighthouse keeper.

A lonely life, sure, but necessary.

But what have I ever prevented from crashing on the rocks?

Truth is, I just drink whiskey on the rocks.

Then I crash.

JOHN GREY 6

John Grey is an Australian born short story writer, poet, playwright, musician, and a Providence RI resident since late seventies. He's been published in numerous magazines including Weird Tales, Christian Science Monitor, Greensboro Poetry Review, Poem, Agni, Poet Lore, *and* Journal of the American Medical Association *as well as the horror anthology* What Fears Become *and the science fiction anthology* Futuredaze. *He has had plays produced in Los Angeles and off, off Broadway in New York. He was the winner of Rhysling Award for short genre poetry in 1999.*

CAROLINE MISNER

HIS HEAD LAY like a shriveled apple, so light it barely made a dent in the green hospital pillow. A lock of feathery white hair fell over one wrinkled eye and I gently brushed it away. I was careful not to disturb him, silly as it seems. My grandfather lay dying and I wanted him to sleep through what would probably be his last day on earth. Machines wheezed and blinked by his bedside and a clear plastic tube snaked into his nostril, so filled with bristly gray hair I was amazed he could breathe at all. Another tube connected his withered arm to a sack of clear fluid that dangled from an intravenous stand by the bed like a plastic umbilical cord. I found it ironic that we come into this world connected by a cord of flesh to our mothers, yet we leave this world tethered by an artificial cord to a machine.

Grandpa moaned and I swear I could hear his neck creak like a rusty hinge as he slowly turned his head and gazed up at me with rheumy eyes. At first, I thought he didn't recognize me, but his furrowed mouth slowly crinkled into a weak smile, showing his one good tooth.

"Toby?" he whispered.

"I'm here," I said and leaned closer so I could hear him.

"Where's your mother?" he croaked.

"She went downstairs to get a bite to eat," I replied. "She'll be back soon."

"Toby," he said and reached out with a trembling hand

speckled with tawny age spots. "How long have I been here?"

"About a week," I replied. His skin felt like cold paper in my hands.

"A week?" His eyes widened with sudden lucidity.

"Don't get so upset, Grandpa," I said. "You need your rest. Just relax."

"Am I dying?" he asked.

His words made my eyes bulge with prickly tears and weighted down my feeble attempt to smile.

"What do doctors know, anyway?" I choked around the nodule in my throat.

"Toby, this is very important." His voice took on a sudden burst of urgency. "I need you to do something for me."

"Anything," I replied.

"I want you to take some food and water to that woman in the park," he said.

"What?" I sat back in my chair. It was the last thing I expected a dying old man to say.

"I know it sounds silly, but it's very important and I can't explain it to you now," he said. "Will you do it?"

"Yes," I stammered. "I guess I could do it."

"Right now," he said. "She's been waiting for me."

"Now?"

"Yes, now." He squeezed my hand surprisingly hard considering his weakened condition.

"But I don't want to leave you," I said. "You shouldn't be alone at a time like this."

"This is more important," he replied. "Her name is Abby. She can explain everything to you once you get there."

I waited until my mother and sister returned to the room before scooping the car keys from her purse.

"Where are you going?" Mom demanded when she saw me snatch my jacket and head for the door.

"Toby's going on a little errand for me." Grandpa winked from his bed.

"I'll be back soon," I assured my mom.

I bought a clubhouse sandwich with a side order of French fries and a large bottle of Evian water from the hospital cafeteria and headed toward the parking lot.

We always wondered who that mysterious woman was. Ever since my grandmother died of cancer ten years ago Grandpa was seen conversing intimately with her and bringing her packages, much to the chagrin of the family. Grandma's ashes were barely in their urn before Grandpa was seen down by the river, a habit he maintained almost every day. When my sister and I were younger, he often brought us down to the spot where the gurgling waters bubbled into the basin of the man-made pond. We would laugh and try to skip stones across the churning surface of the lake while the woman looked on from her spot. He never brought us near her and never introduced us, but often asked us to wave to her from a distance and she would always wave back.

"Who is she?" I asked.

"Just a friend," Grandpa replied and cast a knowing smile in her direction.

Just a friend, I thought as I parked the car and carried the food across the park toward the river. If she was such a good friend, why had he never introduced her to the family? Why was she still standing there alone in the park while he lay dying in the hospital? Why wasn't she at his bedside like my mother and sister and me?

I found her at her usual spot sitting cross-legged on a small patch of emerald green grass and humming an old song to herself. She was absently twirling a yellow flower between two fingers and watching the sun drops gambol across the rippling river.

"Toby, is that you?" she gasped when she saw me approach.

"Do you know me?" I asked. The closer I came to her, the more familiar she looked. The color of her hair and eyes, the curve of her cheek, the arc of her smile, everything about her sent a deluge of cached memories stirring below my consciousness.

She sprung to her feet and smiled like I was a long-lost friend.

"I've known you all your life, Toby," she said. "My name is Abigail—Abby."

"I'm sorry, but I don't remember you," I replied and handed her the paper bag I carried. "My grandfather asked me to bring you this."

"Thank you." Her eyes never left mine as she accepted the bag. "I've been wondering where he is."

"He's not well." Another lump sprouted in my throat. "He's had a stroke and the doctor says it doesn't look like he's going to make it."

Sorrow creased Abby's brow and her lower lip quivered like she was about to cry.

"Poor Glen," she said. "If only he had stayed here with me."

"I don't think there's anything you could have done," I said. "I've brought you some food like he asked me, so if you'll excuse me, I should get back to the hospital and be with him."

"Wait," Abby said as I turned to leave. "Stay with me for a little while. It's been so long since I've seen you. I've missed you

and everyone else in the family. Glen was the only one who came by to see me."

"Are we related?" I asked.

"Yes, we are." She forced a smile through quivering lips. "I'm your grandmother."

"My grandmother is dead." I gritted my teeth so I wouldn't shout. "If you and Grandpa had some sort of thing going on after she died, then that's your business. But it's over now."

"No." Abby shook her head. "It's not like that. Sit here with me for a while and I'll explain everything to you. I know you like to hear stories. I used to tell you all kinds of stories when you were little. Don't you remember?"

"I don't have time for this nonsense," I said and turned to leave again. "My grandpa is on his deathbed."

"Please, Toby," Abby pleaded. She sat back down on the grass and patted a spot directly in front of her. "Just for a little while. It won't take long."

I hesitated. The hospital had become a dismal tomb over the past few days. To be honest, I was slightly relieved that Grandpa had asked me to run this errand; it offered an opportunity to go out and get some air. The thought of returning to that stifling hospital room to watch him wither away like the decomposing corpse he would soon become depressed me, and I was in no hurry to get back.

"Okay," I sighed and sat on the grass in front of her. "Just for a little while, then I really have to get back."

"Thank you, Toby." Abby smiled. "It's so nice to have some company. It gets very lonely here sometimes."

"Then why don't you just leave?" I asked her.

"I wish I could," Abby chuckled. "But that's part of the story."

I sat and listened.

Glen and Abby were dying; they both knew it. Abby had a head start on her husband. She was succumbing to a cancer that was slashing her insides apart like a freshly sharpened razor. Every morning she would awaken to find a mound of white hair on her pillow. Most days she could barely lift herself out of bed to bathe or dress. Sometimes she stayed in bed all day, moaning and thrashing as the chemotherapy worked its way through her system. Glen did his best to help his wife, but his own health was deteriorating, albeit at a slower pace. Arthritis grated his knee joints and stiffened his shoulders so that he was permanently stooped. He had an ulcer that flared whenever he ate anything the least bit spicy or salty, and eventually found himself subsisting on a diet of plain tea and dry toast. They both suffered from cataracts, but neither was well enough to tolerate the surgery required to remove them. They were being methodically strangulated by the tendrils of old age.

Every available surface in their tidy little apartment was occupied with vials and bottles of various medications, some for Glen but most for Abby. There were tablets for his arthritis, capsules for Abby's cancer, more pills to counteract the side effects of the chemotherapy, antibiotics for the infections that resulted from her weakened immune system. Glen stood with his hands in his pockets, staring at the bottles queued in a neat row on the kitchen table. Abby had just taken the last of her medication for the day and was relaxing in the living room in front of the television. Glen sighed, trying to ignore the crick in his neck as he turned his head.

"I'm going out for a walk," he said. "Will you be all right for a while?"

"Fine," Abby replied. "I'm not so bad today."

"That's good," Glen smiled. He knew his wife suffered through bad days and good days; lately the bad days seemed to outnumber the good. "I won't be long. I'm just going to stroll down to the park and get some air."

He wandered down to the large park at the end of their street and followed a path down to the river. It was a glorious spring day. After almost a full week of rain, the clouds had finally split, revealing an azure sky, bright and brilliant and so full of promise that it saddened Glen to think Abby may never see another day like that again. The first of the spring leaves had burst from their chrysalis and splayed across the branches overhead, dappling the sunlight on the path before him. Small clouds of dust puffed up from his sneakers with each painful step. The arthritis in his knees was getting worse and Glen was afraid he would have to either increase his medication or succumb to using a cane.

By the time he reached the riverbank he was panting and clutching his chest. Every joint in his back ached in protest. Ignoring it, Glen turned and decided to press on along the riverbank toward the pond where a group of young boys were racing makeshift boats of folded newspaper.

He thought he was having a stroke. The sensation that overtook him was so sudden and surprising he stopped dead in his tracks, certain he would collapse into a heap on the ground. His vision blurred and Glen realized it was because he didn't need his glasses anymore. He pulled them from his nose and gazed around, seeing the world clearly for the first time in years. The dementia that had recently clogged his mind was gone like dust swept away on a warm breeze. Memories that had long since been buried in his fuddled brain came surging back to him. The pain in his joints had vanished, and he felt lighter and freer than he had in years. He took another step forward, expecting to feel the familiar sting in his knees, surprised that he felt so strong and able. He straightened his spine and stood tall and erect. When he glanced down at his legs he gasped.

His corduroy pants bagged around his thighs and drooped at the waist. He touched his belly, expecting to find that familiar flabby bulge but instead discovered his waist was flat and solid and corrugated with firm muscle. Then he saw his hands. He raised them to his face, unable to believe what he was seeing. Both hands were smoothed of the blue bulging veins that branched out toward his fingers; the thick nodules of his arthritic knuckles were gone, fine black hair sprouted around his wrists.

"I am dreaming?" he whispered to himself and pushed back the thick hair that tumbled down his forehead.

He patted himself up and down the sides of his body and leaned over to peer into the flat, clear surface of the water. The man who gazed back at him was perhaps in his early twenties, certainly no more than thirty; it was a man with a full head of hair and wide muscular shoulders, eyes clear and bright, a smooth complexion devoid of spots or creases. It was the man he used to be.

"This is not possible." He shook his head at his reflection. "I can't be young again."

He stared down at his feet. He was standing on a patch of lime green grass about ten feet in diameter. He reached out into the air in front of himself and felt a tingle against his palm, as though he was pressing against an electrified plastic membrane. He pushed a little harder and his hand popped past the shield. He gasped.

The hand he saw at the end of his arm was spotted and gnarled with age. He felt the familiar ache of arthritis in his knuckles as he bent his fingers. Staring at his hand he realized he was standing within a bubble suspended in time. He pulled back and felt a sensation like an electrical pulse against the skin as it was miraculously transformed back into a young man's hand.

He spent the next hour feeling his way around the inside of the bubble like a mime. He surmised the bubble was perfectly round and about ten feet in diameter, the walls of the membrane meeting exactly at the edge of the patch of grass. Each time he stepped past the threshold of grass he felt his body shrivel and weaken as old age thrust itself upon him like an unwelcome assault.

He thought of Abby and knew exactly what he must do. Rushing home, he found her snoozing on the couch in the living room, clutching a rumpled wad of tissue in one hand.

"Abby, wake up!" He roused her from her slumber and pulled her to her feet.

"What is it?" she croaked groggily.

"I've found the most amazing thing in the park," he said as he draped Abby's coat around her shoulders. "I've no time to explain right now, but I have to show you."

"Can't it wait?" Abby asked as he pushed her toward the door. "I'm not feeling very well right now."

"This can't wait," Glen replied. "It's the most amazing thing you've ever seen."

"But Glen . . ." Abby's voice trailed off weakly as he led her out the door and down the street on wobbly legs.

Twilight was already settling in around the park when they arrived at the river. Abby blinked and peered through her glasses, but she could see nothing extraordinary, just the full moon rising and casting its liquefied image onto the undulating water.

"This way." Glen took her hand and led her toward the grassy patch.

"I don't see anything . . . oh!"

Abby shuddered under the sensation as she stepped through the invisible shield. All vestiges of old age dropped away from her like a serpent shedding its skin. She drew in a cleansing breath, the first deep inhalation she had taken in months. She shook her head and long auburn hair fluttered down over her smooth, curved shoulders.

"Glen!" she said to the familiar young man standing before her. "Is that you?"

"Yes, it's me." Glen smiled and grabbed Abby around the waist.

"What's happened?" Abby gasped and gazed at her own creamy, unblemished hands.

"We're young again!" Glen beamed. "Just like when we were in our twenties."

"But how?" Abby asked. Her housedress hung like an old curtain over her lithe, curvy figure.

"I don't know." Glen shook his head. "I just know that whenever we step into this circle of grass, we're young and healthy again."

"I feel so strong," Abby said and clutched at her narrow waist and full breasts. "Like I haven't been sick a day in my life."

"Me too." Glen nodded and embraced her with more passion than he had felt in twenty years. "This is amazing. We could live forever, suspended in time."

"It's a miracle!" Abby laughed. "Let's go and tell someone. This is too good to keep from the world."

"We can't," Glen sighed. "If you step out of the circle, you're old again. I should know. I've spent half the afternoon stepping in and out of it."

"Then let's stay here forever!" Abby said.

"Forever's a long time," Glen replied.

"I don't care," Abby shook her head. "I can't go back out there again. I couldn't stand to be old and sick anymore. You don't know what it's like; the pain, the chemotherapy, the nausea. I can't go back to that."

"Then I'll stay here with you," Glen smiled and gazed into Abby's eyes, clear of cataracts and shining like orbs of blue crystal.

They made love in the grass until dawn paled the eastern horizon and birds warbled from their nests. As the sun rose they watched the park spring to life with shrieking children and couples strolling hand in hand, young mothers pushing infants in strollers along the path and joggers panting past.

"We're just like them now," Abby sighed and leaned into Glen's firm shoulder.

"Almost," Glen agreed. "We can watch them, we just can't join them."

"I'd rather watch them young than join them old and dying." Abby smiled.

They stayed together, curled in one another's arms, for several days. They found that all time ceased. The bubble remained the same temperature; even at night when the world chilled around them, they could watch the mist rising from the water and dew beading on the leaves and grass, but as long as they remained within the bubble, they stayed warm and content, devoid of any discomfort or hunger or thirst, encased in the warm bubble of time. Each day they watched the world unfold around them, oblivious to the curious glances cast in their direction. Sometimes, a child would approach them if a ball happened to roll in their direction, and Glen would scoop it up and toss it back to the kids with the strength and agility of a seasoned pitcher.

"I can't stay here anymore, Abby," Glen said after several days. A little boy about Toby's age had wondered by and asked Glen to join him in a game of pickle, but Glen had to turn him away.

"Why not?" Abby asked.

"It's too much," Glen shook his head. "Watching all these people enjoy life but being stuck here in this spot. I can't do it any longer."

"But you'll be old and sick if you step out of the circle," Abby said.

"I know," Glen nodded. "It's a sacrifice I'm willing to make. Come with me, Abby. We've had *our fun. It's time to go back to the way we were."*

"No." Abby shook her head and stepped back. "I can't. I won't. I couldn't stand to be like that again."

"Don't be afraid, Abby," Glen extended his hand, but Abby brushed it away.

"I won't go," Abby said. "I want to stay here where I can be young and healthy. It would kill me to step outside the circle now."

"I can't leave you," Glen said.

"Then don't." Abby tugged at his arm. "Stay here with me."

"But I can't do that either," Glen replied. "I miss our daughter and our grandchildren."

"I miss them, too," Abby said. "But I can't go back out there again. I just can't!"

"Abby, please . . ."

"No!"

"But you will be all alone." Glen sighed.

"I can't go back to the way I was before." Abby's eyes brimmed with tears. "I just can't. You go ahead. I'd rather stay here, even if it means being without you."

"Are you sure?"

"Go," Abby said. "I'll stay here."

"I'll come visit you every day," Glen said.

"I'll be waiting."

Glen kissed his wife and stepped off the grassy patch. Abby wept softly as she watched his hunched body painfully shuffle up the path and disappear into the encroaching night.

I stared at Abby. She was smirking back at me as though defying me to believe what I had just heard.

"That's impossible," I said. "My grandmother died. I went to the funeral with my mother and sister. I remember it like it was yesterday."

"Glen told the family that I had suc-cumbed to the cancer," Abby said and shook her head thoughtfully. "He bought an urn and filled it with sand and held a small memorial service for me at your mother's house. I wish I could have been there. It must be something to be present at your own funeral."

Abby didn't flinch as I lifted my hand and pressed it toward her. Sure enough, I felt a slight resistance tingle against my palm like a plastic film just at the breaking point. It burst through and I stared at my own hand within the bubble.

"But I'm the same," I said and gently touched her shoulder.

"Of course you are." Abby smiled and covered my hand with her own and kissed the knuckles. "You're already young. It only seems to work on those who really need it, the old and infirm."

"This is incredible," I gasped and drew my hand back.

"I know," Abby agreed.

"I'll be right back!" I surged to my feet.

"Where are you going?" Abby asked.

I didn't reply. I bolted across the park to the car. I knew exactly what to do; hopefully I could get to the hospital before it was too late and get past the nurses and orderlies undetected.

Grandpa had lapsed into another fitful slumber by the time I arrived in his room. Mom was dozing in a chair in the corner and my sister was gnawing a wad of gum and absently flipping through the pages of a magazine. I made some feeble excuse to get them out of the room, assuring them that I would watch over Grandpa and call them if he took a turn for the worse.

He felt like a loose sack of chicken bones in my arms. Tubes and wires dangled from his flaccid body, and I yanked them out before scooping him up and rushing toward the door. I covered him with several layers of blankets and implored him not to make a sound. From a distance I looked like someone carrying a load of laundry out to a car idling patiently near the rear entrance.

I bundled Grandpa into the back seat and begged him to keep his head down and not make a sound. Ten minutes later, we were back at the park. Grandpa had lapsed into semi-consciousness by then.

"What are you doing?" Grandma gasped when she saw me approach.

"I've brought Grandpa," I replied. "Hurry. Take him. We don't have much time. I think he's in a coma."

"Glen?" Grandma gazed down at the shriveled remains of her husband. His wizened head flopped against the crook of my elbow; a light breeze lifted a wispy lock of hair from his brow, as light and white as milkweed.

"Take him in with you," I said and tried to pass the bundle over to her.

"No!" Abby had tears drizzling down her cheeks. She stepped back with both hands raised as though surrendering to a gunman.

"What?"

"It's not what he wanted," Abby said. "He wanted to live his life and die in peace."

"Are you crazy?" I shouted. "He's dying! Take him before it's too late."

"I can't." Abby shook her head.

"I don't have time to argue," I said. "Take him!"

Grandpa shuddered and groaned in my arms. I could feel the life ebbing away from him.

"You were right, Glen," Abby said. "Immortality is not worth the price. I'll go with you."

Abby stepped forward. She collapsed at my feet like a macerated mannequin before I could stop her—a wizened old woman with wild gray hair.

Grandpa lifted his head from my shoulder and whispered, "Abby?"

Tears stung my eyes as I laid his body down on the grass beside his wife. They reached out to one another, their fingers touching softly, as together they drew their last breaths in this world.

Caroline Misner's work has appeared in numerous publications in the USA, Canada, India and the UK. She has been nominated for the prestigious McClelland & Stewart Journey Anthology Prize for the short story "Strange Fruit"; in 2011 another short story and a poem were nominated for the Pushcart Prize. She lives in the beautiful Haliburton Highlands of Northern Ontario where she continues to draw inspiration for her work. She is the author of the Young Adult fantasy series "The Daughters of Eldox". Her latest novel, "The Spoon Asylum" was released in May of 2018 by Thistledown Press and has been nominated for the Governor General Award.

GOSSAMER FIELDS

JACKSON SMITH

SEATED BEHIND HIS mahogany double pedestal desk —which he had bought for a pretty penny from Valentino Design on La Cienega—Bird Weems thought about a place he hated to remember. For fifteen years, he'd done his best to forget Idaho, forget the cold, forget the crippling ranching that had done its best to turn his hands into gnarled wood. Now, trying to find the ocean through sky-scrapers and smog, he felt the many hairy legs of his past prickle down his shirt collar.

He turned Clara-Sue Weems's letter, his Gam's letter, over and over in his fingers, a talismanic practice to calm and kill time until guilt forced his hand. Fifteen years come and gone. Fifteen years since he hitched the moonlit I-15 from Kilgore to Los Angeles. And what a fifteen years they'd been. Clarence Weems from Kilgore was now Bird Weems from East Hollywood. Head of his own content house. Head of Bird Productions.

Back when he was running desks at CESD, there was a regular joke that Clarence ate his hams and cheeses like "a friggin' stork." And they weren't wrong; even in Kil-gore people had made fun of his long legs and sunken chest. But Kilgore was a long way away. So were the names Clarence, Clay, Cal, and Larry. He knew that the name Bird was meant to be punitive, but just like every pile of shit he'd ever shoveled, he accepted it. From then on, he was Bird. Bird Weems.

Once more he turned the letter with his fingers. *Clarence* was written across the front in the quagmire of his Gam's cursive. Nobody but Gam called him Clarence. With a deep breath and a sterling silver letter opener, he let forth the spiders.

Dear Clarence,

I know we haven't talked in some time, but I still have great affection for you and am not angry. On the contrary, I saw an ad with your face on it in the Jefferson Star (though I do not know what it was doing there) and could not be prouder.

Bird himself had put it there to inform the lowly pig eaters of Clark County how far he'd come.

It was always very clear to me that you were born much too big for Kilgore. Though I never said it, I have always felt that you were a son to me, and I hoped (and still hope) that you view me as a mother. Now that I have said that, I will do my best not to let sentimentality get in the way of what's to come, as I have a few pieces of information that I wish to relay.

I suppose that I will start with the easy piece first. My time is coming to an end, Clarence. I can feel my lungs tightening, and I have no doubt that the cancer has already set its hooks in me. My ma went the same way, as did my sister. It simply cannot be helped. When your time comes, I am sure you will understand. Things being as they are, I have set about the preparation of my will. Clarence, there are some things that never come easy to a parent, and I imagine this is one of them.

Bird's damp fingers marked the page.

You will not be receiving the ranch when I die. There is no doubt in my mind that this will cause you anger (it has not been so long that I have forgotten your temperament), and

I promise that I do not do this out of spite or anger. And I suppose this brings me to my next point.

A number of years ago a man by the name of Arno Crase entered my life. Mr. Crase is a kind man, kinder than any man I have met. As a young man, he roamed the land as a traveling minister, spreading the good word to the humble folks of our fair nation. This may be hard for you to hear, Clarence, but I love him, and he will be inheriting the ranch after I pass on. He is calling them, Clarence, calling them all. How wonderful would that be, Clarence? A haven for the crushed and downtrodden, here on our little ranch. Forgive me, I have slipped into the sentimentality I so tried to avoid. You may hate me for this, but just know that I love you, son. I love you and I miss you. Please do not come try and change my mind. Be well.

With Love,
Clara-Sue Weems

Bird wondered at the tinny, wobbling sound that filled the room like vibrating glass and realized briefly that it was not, in fact, in the room. The glass was in his ears and was filling his head from the inside, expanding in shape and tenor against his eyes and the front of his skull. Then he noticed the red droplets coloring Gam's letter. He let the bloody letter opener drop from his hand.

Arno Crase. Or maybe it was Father Arno Crase. For Bird, it didn't matter if it were King Arno Crase of Siam. It didn't matter because names were not important to dead men. And Mr. Crase was certainly a dead man. Deader than Disco.

"Crystal? I need you!" Bird yelled.

The large breasted blonde opened the door, eyes wide as if she could somehow divine Bird's demands by power of sight.

"I need you to book me the earliest flight you can to Idaho Falls."

"Mr. Weems, you have a 12:30 with CBS tomorrow."

"Question, Crystal. Do you run this office? Because last time I checked it was my name out there and not yours." His smile was humorless.

"Sorry, Mr. Weems." Her eyes fell at the coldness in his voice.

He'd have to fall on his sword for missing the meeting, but he could think about that later. Now, he had a Crase to fry. "Just make the reservation. I'll handle the rest."

The door shut with a bang, leaving Bird in silence. A thin line of copper blood flowed down Bird's wrist, bronzing the cuff of his Canali cotton.

Under the pastel orange of an Idaho sunset, Bird's soon-to-be ranch house sat back about a half-mile from the road, a long pathway of red volcanic cinders leading to the front door. Bird had taken the 7:50 out of LAX to Idaho Falls, then sped like a madman, nearly running two separate vehicles off the road. Now he was here and couldn't remember how he'd managed to bear it for so many years. Much less why he was fighting to keep it. All he knew was that Arno Crase was in for the ride of his life.

A whitewash of silken webs covered the fields of bluestem and crested wheatgrass like drifts of snow under the setting sun. Gam had said the webs were a biological phenomenon, said that in times of heavy rain spiders created these sorts of suspended pathways between whatever nesting poles they'd staked out in order to avoid the flood, but he

could only ever recall about two rainstorms in his life. Perhaps they had a taste for clean air.

Bird inhaled.

Damn if the air wasn't crisper up here. No cars, no traffic, no smog. No work either.

He took his first steps down the scoria pathway, pumice edges audibly scraping on each step. He was *Bird* through and through: his steps were elongated and loping, as if he were constantly stepping over puddles of water or refuse.

From what he could see, the ground beneath the web was still deeply furrowed by the maze-like pattern of writhing gopher mounds. Gam letting the gophers run like this? She really *was* sick. Past the house, the white fields stretched as far as he could see.

Looking left and right, Bird tried to let the landscape wash over him, center him before he arrived, but it seemed now that the webs smothered more than they ever had. Once upon a time, he'd loved this place, the way the morning sun set fire to the thistle and brome, the way his Gam had left out evening scraps for the raccoons and coyotes that tore huge swathes through the white fields. This was a far cry from the City of Angels, hell, from a city of *anything*. But it was his, damn it, and he'd be damned if he'd let some dink preacher take it from him. For Christ's sake, he'd fenced this whole pathway with lay-down four-wire barb, so the fence wouldn't collapse during winter snow. All around him, the white webs reflected the cotton candy sun, fading from orange to purple.

Looking at the fence as he neared the house, scoria still crunching underneath, a question rose in his chest. Maybe he'd grown unaccustomed to the soft cotton ooze, but the whole landscape seemed less defined, the surroundings more web than flora, the diaphanous mess growing thicker the closer he came to the house. Were there more webs here than before? If anything he'd thought that there would be *fewer* webs, that his mind had magnified the landscape in his years away.

He supposed it was just paranoia, but he couldn't shake the feeling that there was something different. Something worse in the air and soil. He looked out to the east and saw webs like thick mist coating the barbed wire fence. Everything was stock-still.

No, this was wrong. It couldn't be still; nothing was ever stock-still on this path. As a kid he would've had to shake loose the spiders from his hair by this point. Where the hell were they?

Bird balked at the thought of the spiders' absence. After all, he didn't fear their bite or venom; he knew that the majority were impotent little-mouthed bastards that prickled more than pounced. But they crept in the night as one, and more than once, he'd had to pull them from his socks or underwear. They weren't just predators, they were a force of nature: a tsunami, omnipresent and indefatigable, that woke him in the middle of the night, that slid in between the folds of his brain, filled his mind like the dry engine burn of a cocaine comedown.

And now that he was back and they were gone, the ranch seemed to lack a certain vitality; perhaps if he'd had time, or a clearer head, he might've noticed the lack of birds, the flicker of insects, the dead silence.

To his left rested an old bicycle. His old bicycle. A patina of age and rust. Had he been gone so long as to forget his youth? A teenage boy, all knees and ankles, pushing a rusted, sea-green bicycle up the volcanic road in the dead of night; an old woman stamping out gopher mounds wearing her special order LL Bean mosquito bucket hat (specially modified at the netting's base for arachnids); periods of respite after hot afternoons of work on the screened-in porch, damp t-shirt like a second skin.

Then, at the circular drive at the end of walk, Bird saw his target. Arno Crase, the holy man. Arno Crase, The Usurper. Only he didn't seem holy to Bird—he didn't seem powerful enough to usurp anything. Crase was a cripple. A crip they'd have called him in a bygone era. And there he was, a black shadow against the sunset, straddling the line between rock and web.

Goddamn his Gam and her goodness. In a whipsnap of thought, Bird got it. Kind old maid that she was, it made complete sense that this wheel-bound shyster had been able to inveigle the ranch out of his hands. She hadn't meant to rob Bird, not at all. She'd been tricked, duped by this charlatan. Besides the gophers, whose mounds she had smashed indiscriminately, Bird literally could not remember his Gam committing an unkind act. Leave it to the malice of a crippled preacher to con an old woman out of her property.

Almost as if Crase could sense his thoughts, he turned and began to wheel toward Bird, hand raised in greeting. How do you negotiate with a crip? Certainly not the way you negotiate with the top desk at CBS. You had to play it cool, not let the man know you felt any pity, any disgust. Promote a shade of equality. Only then, when you were on equal footing, could you upend him.

Bird's mind went blank the moment Crase rolled up and offered his hand, the sounds of the tired rubber on the volcanic cinders ceasing as he came to a stop. Bird shook his

hand. Never before had a figure imposed such a sense of incongruity. The man's legs were terribly atrophied beneath his checkered blanket, dangling limply like a marionette's limbs. His hands were unyielding, strangely engorged beneath Bird's grip, and Bird wondered if his hands had been afflicted by whatever ailed his lower half.

"Oh my, oh my. What a surprise," Crase said.

Bird's eyes widened. Sweet Harry Houdini. That voice. Deep, golden: it made no sense to Bird how such a resonant voice could come from such a feeble man. In that moment, hand in waxen hand, Bird was very aware of how alone he was, and for the most slender second he thought that maybe, just maybe, this crip standing in front of the spider field was dangerous, and that he should run, just forget everything up to this point, and run back to LA where things were always as they seemed and there were no mad preachers north of Orange County. But then it was too late. Arno Crase was speaking.

"You must be Clarence. And you do so look like her," a small twinkle shone in Crase's eye, as if he were genuinely excited to see Bird.

"It's Bird actually," Crase released his hand, then, "I go by Bird."

"Forgive me, Clara-Sue never mentioned that. You must've picked it up after you moved out."

Moved out, not ran away. Clever.

"Where is she?" Bird asked.

"I imagine she's gussying up." Crase wheeled an inch closer to Bird. "Look here, son. There's no doubt in my mind that you're here to discuss the property, but is there a chance we could do it after supper? Clara-Sue and I usually sup around now and I'd be most grateful if you'd join us."

"Of course," Bird replied. How on earth could he say no.

"Thank you much. I truly appreciate it, Clarence." *It's Bird you wheel-bound clown. Bird.*

Crase pulled away, motioning for Bird to follow.

Remember the rules they taught you at CESD? Control the conversation, but do it subtly. Don't give the opposing party reason to speak out. Keep them off balance, but provide amenities. Somehow Crase had managed the whole gamut without even standing up.

There was another rule, however, a rule that Bird had forgotten: don't underestimate your opponent.

"It's been quite a while since I've seen the old lady," Bird said, following Crase. Whether he meant the house or his Gam, Bird wasn't sure.

All around him the webs grew tighter, and finding Crase a tougher opponent than he was expecting, with his Bing-Crosby-over-rocks voice, the uncertainty in Bird's stomach began to expand. He entered the house and the screen door closed behind him, sending echoes through the darkening land.

Gam's kitchen was exactly as he recalled. The same green striped tablecloth, the same tomato-red cabinets, the same soft-streak linoleum. Except now, Crase sat at the head instead of his Gam. Bird was thankful the man had tucked his ruined legs under the table.

"It sure is cozy in here, Clarence, and it sure is good to finally meet you. Clara-Sue has told me much about you."

"That so?" Stupid, Bird. Stupid. Petulance is for children.

"It is. I have acted as tender ear on many occasions. I believe, before my arrival of course, that she was terribly lonely. It can be hard to speak with spiders as your only audience." Crase chuckled quietly. Damn it. Even his laugh is melodic.

"You know, Mr. Crase—"

"It's Father Crase, if you don't mind, son."

"Well, Father Crase," the words nearly caught in Bird's throat, "I respect hospitality in a man. I really do. But I came here to talk to my Gam, so where is she?"

"When last I checked she was tending to something upstairs. Clara-Sue?" He called out. Nothing. The creak of old wheels. Crase turned his head back to Bird. "I find that sometimes, when she sets her mind to a chore, there's nothing but the sweet lord himself that can pry her away from it. You know how she is."

A lull now. Here's your chance. Control the conversation.

"You know this place isn't worth much, father. Can't grow anything. Sure as hell can't build anything. Not with the spiders," Bird said.

"Be that as it may, the land suits my needs quite nicely," Crase smiled.

"Yeah? What needs would those be?"

"I'm creating a sanctuary, Clarence," his smile widened and he tented his fingers. The sight made Bird uneasy.

"With all these spiders? You're kidding yourself if you think anyone's going to come *here.*"

"I take it you're not a fan of spiders, Clarence. Not an arachnid fanatic. Well there's nothing wrong with that."

Unsure of what to say, Bird looked at his hands.

"Spiders are the world's underdogs. They are the watchers that keep the worst from the door. Centipedes, wasps, cockroaches: all fall prey to the eyes of the spider. Without spiders, the world would be overrun by flies, by pestilence. And do we appreciate them? *No,*" Crase slammed his fist down onto the green tablecloth. "All we have for the noble spider is a crush, a kick, a newspaper. No *thank you*, no *come again*, no nothing. Believe me when I tell you, Clarence, no one has it harder than the spider."

"What are you doing here, Crase?" Bird asked.

"I am trying to found a haven, in a world ruled by nonbelievers. And it's father Crase, Clarence."

Bird couldn't take it anymore. So high and mighty, so holier than thou, so wheelbound on his soapbox. But Bird saw through it. Saw through his land-grabbing bullshit.

"You're going to have to build your paradise elsewhere, *Father* Crase, because this is my home."

"You treat your home like this, Clarence? You don't visit, you don't call, you don't even bother to write. After all Clara-Sue did for you, Clarence."

Bird looked down and realized he was clenching his fists; little white crescents pressed into his palm.

"My name's not Clarence, you crip son of a whore. It's Bird. And it takes a real man to handle a ranch like this."

A smile played at the corner of Crase's mouth. Bird did not look away from the preacher's eyes.

"I know my 'crip' body lacks the mobility of a real farm boy like you," Crase laughed to himself, as if he knew something Bird didn't, "but after years of loneliness, Clara-Sue seemed to think that *anybody* here was better than nobody. Real man or not."

Bird was standing now, rounding the table.

This last jab was unsupportable.

He loomed over the crippled Crase. "I don't know what you plan on doing with this place, but you don't deserve it. You haven't worked for it. Yeah, maybe it's scarier than a goddamn graveyard, but it's *mine*."

"Clarence, Clarence. I have grander plans for this place than you could possibly imagine. I am His chosen priest, and it is my duty to summon them, to unite them like the lost tribes of Israe—"

"Oh that's right, *Father* Crase. Forgot you were an oh-so-holy man, bent on delivering the good word on whatever it is you preach. Well I'm not buying it. You can take your hoodoo, pseudo-religious occult mumbo jumbo, and you can jam it up your ass."

Crase's voice turned from soft gold to molten metal, filling the room like the climax of a sermon.

"You will hold your tongue, boy! You may besmirch me and my damaged body all you like, but I will not sit idly by while you befoul the name of my chosen god."

Without realizing, Bird took a step back, shocked by the impact of Crase's fervor. Crase rolled forward, and Bird's eyes were immediately pulled to the outline of Crase's shriveled limbs.

"You made your choice fifteen years ago, young man, and there's nothing you can do to change that."

Bird opened his mouth, closed it. What could he say? "Where the hell is she?" Bird said.

Crase paused for a moment, then let slip his golden tongue. "Come to say, Clarence, I remember her saying something about a chore in the basement. Perhaps you could check down there and see if she'll be joining us for supper?"

In every negotiation, there was a time to call the bluff, to throw down your cards and say *here's my hand, now show me what you got.* This was Bird's. He hoped against hope that he had chosen the right time. Moreover, he hoped that there was a right time and that the cold fear in his belly was just active paranoia and that the, *fuck everything and go far, far from here* instinct was not in fact instinct, but a case of the jitters. Bird wanted to run—the cold ball in his gut was telling him to run—but like before, Bird looked into the man's eyes and knew that he could not run, *would* not run. This was his Gam, and she might be in trouble. This was his house, and it might be brought to ruin; he'd be damned if he'd let some creepy old preacher take them from him.

Bird walked left past Crase out of the kitchen and opened the door to the basement. A dim flicker emanated from the depths, not providing enough light to see, just enough to temper the fear. He walked into the half-light.

As he flicked the lights at the base of the stairs, the first great horror of his life wrapped him with sticky fibers. He did not notice the rusty red toolkit, inside of which he used to hide his pornos and cigarettes. He did not notice the shelf full of pickled rutabagas and peppers he had preserved so long ago with his Gam. But he did notice her. He noticed his Gam.

Stuck against the basement's far wall, she had been cocooned toe to neck, and was now suspended some three feet above the ground, only her gray head sticking out from the white swathe like a small child in a white sleeping bag. Small holes, each a few inches in diameter, honeycombed the wall.

Suddenly Bird was aware of a high-pitched shriek filling the room. He looked left, then right, then it dawned on him; *he* was the source of the noise himself. Forcing himself to be quiet, he ran to her and began to tear at the oily strands, thicker and ropier than the normal webs, all the while perilously afraid that something would come spilling from one of the black holes.

"It's no use, Clarence. You'll never get her out of there."

Bird heard the man's voice, warm and mesmerizing. Surely a crip like him would be stuck at the top of the stairs, rendered impotent by his oldest foe: his own body. But Crase was not at the top of the stairs when Bird looked.

Bird felt something fall directly behind him. A gut reaction, he turned. On the ground there was a hand, a waxy, lifeless hand. He looked up, and that was when he received the day's second great horror.

Spread out against the ceiling was a fleshy blue-black spider with the head of Arno Crase. In a moment of mad clarity Bird realized that Crase's legs had not been shriveled by polio but were four arachnoid branches taped together to present the illusion of decrepitude, and his hands weren't unyielding nerve damaged pieces of dying flesh, they were props, carefully masquerading below the unsuspecting eye. Yet his head, his head was that of a man. It was still Arno Crase's head, but instead of a neck, there was only a thin black stalk bulging with veins. In the blink of an eye, Crase dropped from the ceiling, pinning Bird to the ground with his foul, dark bulk.

"I have a question for you, Clarence. Are you ready for it?"

Bird didn't answer, his mind paralyzed by fear and Crase's hot breath, venomous and golden. Crase's weight was horrible, unyield-

ing and hairy. Slowly, Crase moved one of his hairy forelegs under Bird's chin, moving Bird's jaw up and down like a slack-jawed puppet.

"There we go. My question is: who is the crip now, Clarence? You, or us?"

As Crase uttered this last word he pressed Bird's temple to the side, forcing him to look left.

Spiders of all shapes and colors, of all sizes and venoms, erupted from the holes in the wall like a great black flood. Torrential they fell, skittering down the walls like the run-off from a waterfall. In seconds they were on Bird, holding him against the ground, like a hairy black blanket. Despite all his years living amidst a sea of silk, Bird had never become accustomed to the hydraulic fluidity of a spider clambering down his body.

They're using the gopher mounds as transport, bird realized madly. They've been moving around under the earth.

"If you ask me, it would seem that *you're* the crip now."

Bird tried to lift up his arm, but felt the needle hot pincers of ten thousand fangs piercing his flesh. He screamed out.

"*I* am not a crip, Clarence. I am of the Tsuchigumo, I am the great prophet of Anansi, and I am the second coming of Queen Mother Arachne."

As Bird looked into the spider preacher's face, he noticed that the nearly human incisors were growing longer, dripping with cloudy bile he could only assume was venom.

"I have crept from Galilee to Golgotha in search of Him, with nothing to show for it but dust in my hair. The gods of this earth are everywhere and I am a pantheon's humble servant."

A blotch of fire spread down Bird's cheek as venom dripped from Crase's incisor, and he noted with worry that the magma had subsided in his leg. It was growing numb.

"You gave me quite the scare today, Clarence. I would never have let your Clara-Sue send that letter if I had known *you* would be the result. You were not supposed to be here. Oh, but she is a clever old bird, I'll give her that."

It was a cry for help. Gam must've known that nothing would've kept Bird away once he learned he was losing the property, she was counting on it.

"You've been holding her prisoner," Bird said.

"Call it what you like," Crase replied. His golden voice had an edge to it. "But she has an opportunity to be a part of something greater than herself. She will be the All-Mother, the homeland of my progeny. You," even longer grew Crase's incisors, obscene and protruding in Crase's human mouth, "you will be nothing more than my brood's first meal, an insignificant worm in the dusty basement of your worn out homestead. Perhaps I should say *my* worn out homestead." Crase drew even closer, nostrils flaring in anticipation.

S. arborea. S. clypeata. A. affinis. The words came to Bird's mind like premonitions. Despite the useless leg and the smell of poison on his face, Bird was fourteen again, stuck in biology class on a cracked plastic stool, the green-covered *Life*, a Mcgraw Hill number, on the black table in front of him. On the blackboard, Mrs. Kinksy was squeaking out the avian species native to Idaho. *S. clypeata*, the Northern Shoveler, *A. affinis*, the Lesser Scaup, and of course, there was *S. arborea*, the American Tree Sparrow. Why was this important? How the hell were these rats with wings important?

Then it clicked for Bird. The key. What do all birds have in common? An appetite for spiders.

As Crase lowered his mouth, Bird met him halfway. Like Crase, his jaws were extended, hungry, but Bird's were tighter, overpowering. Crase's nose crumbled underneath Bird's bite, the tendons and cartilage ripping between his beak, black ichor flooding his mouth. Crase shrieked, recoiling. His army of spiders went wild, freeing Bird from their many-legged embrace as they scattered haphazardly, troops without command. And then Crase's obscene weight lifted, and the spider preacher was rolling on his back, legs constricting and loosening like a clenching fist.

But Bird wasn't done. He was *C. Bird Weems*, spider eater and vanquisher of false prophets. In a fit of frenzy, Bird climbed atop Crase's engorged abdomen, lowered his head, and sunk his teeth into the soft jelly of Crase's eyes.

"If you weren't a crip before, well you damn well are now, you hairy son of a bitch," Bird yelled, viscous jelly dripping down his chin.

Again, Crase shrieked, sending his congregation deeper into mayhem.

Before Crase could recover, Bird lunged awkwardly and tore his Gam down from the wall, hoisted her over his shoulder and set for the stairs.

"Don't let them escape!" Crase yelled, and suddenly Bird knew the arachnid hoard had regained order. He wobbled up the stairs, made it through the kitchen and into the dark night. Taking a sharp right, Bird almost floundered, offset by the cocooned mass on his left shoulder and his useless leg, but he righted himself and continued down the volcanic road, each stride more kinked than the last.

On either side, the Gossamer Fields stretched for miles, but Bird knew that they were empty. All of the spiders were behind him. Like ember heat on his back, Bird heard Crase's voice.

He turned to look.

Standing atop a flood of black movement, Crase forced his way through the front door, his abdomen sticking a brief moment in the frame. For a maddening moment Bird imagined an eighty-foot Crase towering above him like some horrific float transported by an army of spiders.

"Just leave her, Clarence," Crase yelled, "Leave her like you did all those years ago."

Bird tightened his grasp on Gam and kept running, willing movement into the club foot that trailed behind him.

"No matter how far you run, you'll never get those years back."

The spiders were still fifty feet away when Bird arrived at the SUV's passenger door and opened it, frantically trying to unstick Gam's webbing from his shoulder so he could put her into the car. Then spiders were thirty feet away, then twenty, all the while Crase's multi-legged frame growing larger and larger. Sweat fell into Bird's eyes as he jerked and yanked. Ten feet away, then Bird tore off his shirt and closed Gam into the passenger seat. Five feet away and Bird was driving into the night, leaving them forty feet away, then eighty, then too far to count. Even as he fled into the night, Bird heard Crase's voice pursuing endlessly, like a gout of flame across the sky.

Eighteen miles later Bird pulled to the side of the road and pried Gam from the passenger seat, sprigs of web sticking to the leather as she came loose. He laid her on the ground and felt her face. The vaguest hint of warmth.

"Oh, Gam," he said. And there was so much more to say, so much he had been too afraid to say since he'd abandoned her, so much he *needed* to say. He'd hated Crase because he'd been right, but there was time now, time to fix what he'd been too stupid to see earlier.

Nothing. Then a cough, an old body racking, trapped air fighting to be free. He pulled open the webbing surrounding her chest and lowered his head. Movement. Pounding movement. He held her to his chest.

"Hey there, Clarence."

Just for the moment, it was Clarence and his Gam, alone together in the spider fields of Idaho.

When asked about the biographical information in this post, Jackson Smith replied, "Well, I imagine it'll be pretty hard to get the scope of me in 100 words, so maybe just stick to the basics." To that end, Jackson Smith is an aspiring writer. He graduated from Grinnell College with a Bachelor's in English in 2018 and is currently pursuing a graduate degree in Creative Writing from the University of Nebraska at Omaha. If writing doesn't work out, he's thinking about becoming a professional Overwatch player (he also loves video games). His future is uncertain.

LOST AND FOUND

MARTIN LOCHMAN

DISTINGUISHED COLLEAGUES AND scholars!

It is an utmost honor for me to be standing before you today. Before I begin, I wish to extend gratitude and appreciation to the World Scholarly Council for inviting me to this conference, and to my dear friend and colleague, Professor Sestron Sya Saratan who—as you are undoubtedly aware—tragically passed away during his expedition to the Paadrits Mountains two cycles ago. His death represents an immeasurable loss to the scientific community; however, it is my singular intention to commemorate his life's work and bring forth his latest findings, gathered during the expedition.

Professor Saratan dedicated his career to searching for intelligent life beyond our world. He was convinced that it was impossible for our civilization to be the only one of its kind, wholly unique, in such a vast expanse that is the known cosmos. His well-structured theories and hypotheses, widely known and respected amongst his peers, concerned not only the existence of such civilizations on other worlds but also their visits on ours.

Professor Saratan's expedition, launched four cycles ago following unusual seismic activity in the Paadrits Mountains, had one goal—to bring back what always eluded his efforts: the definitive, indisputable proof that his theories were indeed correct.

Words cannot describe how incredibly proud I am to tell you that the expedition has been successful.

In my presentation today, I wish to not only show you several items—or artifacts, if you will—recovered by the surviving members of Professor Saratan's expedition (artifacts that, without a shadow of a doubt, did not originate on our world), but also provide you with evidence that the Professor himself came close to making direct contact with otherworldly beings.

Please! Please allow me to conduct the presentation first! I will answer all your questions at the end, thank you! I greatly appreciate your interest.

Let us begin then.

The first item—as you can see on the images behind me—is a hollow object of a very unusual shape, symmetrical around its central axis. It is 3 zenars long and weighs 6,5 kartks. Throughout most of its length—2,2 zenars to be exact—it bears a cylindrical shape with a diameter of 0,5 zenars, which is significantly narrowed on one end to a diameter of 0,1 zenars. Its end is blunt and has a diameter of 0,1 zenars. The object is made out of an unidentified synthetic material that is solid and extremely resistant to corrosion and degradation by nearly all chemical compounds. Its surface is uniform—without any dents or ridges—and at first glance, it seems completely closed; however, at the smaller end, an opening can be found. Inside, a smaller cylinder—composed of a softer material that appears to be of an organic origin—is firmly lodged, forming an airtight barrier of a sort.

I believe the object to be a container or a mobile storage. In fact, my colleagues in the laboratory were able to penetrate the barrier and uncover that it is almost entirely filled with an unknown liquid substance. With the analysis still ongoing, it is too soon to make any conclusions regarding the purpose of the liquid; however, preliminary results indicate the presence of alkar—which could mean that it is, in fact, a consumable; a beverage perhaps.

The second item appears to be some kind of a machine or device. It is considerably smaller than the container—only 0,9 zenars long with an average diameter of 0,3 zenars, weighing at 1,2 kartks—and far more streamlined in comparison. A thin outer shell, made from a different type of synthetic material that is lighter and more susceptible to corrosion, degradation, and physical damage, protects the complex and intricate machinery inside which is much more advanced than any of our contemporary devices.

Its exact purpose remains a mystery for now, as we haven't been able to make it operational. This may be due to any number of reasons—depleted power source, damage to its critical components, environmental conditions, or other factors. However, given the fact that the machinery protrudes through the protective shell on one end—like so—I would venture to guess that it is a highly sophisticated tool.

The next item—1,6 zenars long and weighing 1,1 kartks—differs greatly from the previous two in both physical characteristics and assumed purpose. It is extremely interesting to note that it consists of a single piece of solid matter, molded into a specific, highly asymmetrical shape. Much like the cylindrical barrier lodged inside of the aforementioned first object, the material of this item also seems to be organic: a natural composite with a porous and fibrous structure. This reflects on its lower density and weight, and higher susceptibility to degradation by chemicals and environmental conditions.

To understand the item's purpose, we need to focus on its surface. As you can see, it is covered with shallow dents that appear random at first, and as such, can be quickly dismissed as damage, but a closer look reveals an organized pattern transcending the asymmetrical shape. A valued colleague of mine, Professor Kvar, suggested we assume a more philosophical point of view when examining the item, which allowed me to draw a conclusion that it doesn't indeed have any practical purpose. Instead, it is of a high cultural, psychological, or emotional significance. If my presumption is correct, this could mean that these beings, albeit advanced beyond imagination, share certain similarities with our own civilization!

The following items have been discovered together in a closed sack with thin, soft, transparent walls resembling an organic membrane. Our analysis uncovered, however, that it is composed of a similar synthetic material to the one making up the protective shell of the unknown device.

The sac held a total of three individual objects. They are identical to each other—closed cylindrical containers (once again made from a similar type of the synthetic material), 0,5 zenars long and 0,2 in diameter. Although the content of every container is uniform—spherical and spherocylindrical pellets of dense inorganic and organic matter—they differ in the quantity, which impacts their individual weights. The presence of organic elements in the pellets could point towards them being consumables; however, as we lack information about the biology of the otherworldly beings, an absolute conclusion cannot be made.

This brings the first part of my presentation to an end. In the second segment, I wish to introduce an acoustic recording made by Professor Saratan himself which documents the presence of these beings. It is crucial to note that certain parts of the recording were irreversibly corrupted prior to its discovery, thus leaving blank spots; nevertheless, much of what the Professor says can be clearly heard. Furthermore, the acoustic document captures a fragment of what is clearly a conversation between two of the beings, making it the most important piece of evidence to date! Of course, their language, intonation, and pronunciation are completely different from any known dialects so nothing can be understood as of yet, but I have the utmost faith that we will be able to understand it in the foreseeable future.

Now, without further ado, I will play the recording:

```
. . . this is truly extraordinary. An enormous object, a machine—by
my estimations at least six hundred zenars long—has just descended
from the atmosphere not far from the site. I wish I could capture this
on an image but it is dark [missing passage] couldn't discern any-
thing. This is the first time in our history that we . . .

[missing passage]

. . . and they are much larger and heavier than us. They appear to
possess only two pairs of limbs—one to propel themselves forward on
the surface and the second, visibly shorter and weaker, to manipulate
```

various objects. One would consider this to be a very inefficient design but witnessing them move with such grace refutes the notion completely.

The beings are clearly interested in the site and the items that we have discovered. They seem to be in constant verbal communication with each other, but their language doesn't sound like anything I have ever heard before. Still, I have to make contact; perhaps they will be able to understand me, given their technological superiority . . .

[missing passage]

. . . they are only about thirty zenars away. I think they can see me now.

"Greetings! My name is Professor Sestron Sya Saratan and it is my honor to welcome you to . . ."

[missing passage]

Please allow me a brief interruption here. Despite being largely incomplete, the recording helps us establish a basic description of the beings. They are large bipedal creatures—although their exact dimensions are unknown—who utilize a very similar system of verbal communication as we do. Furthermore, Professor Saratan's first words allow us to answer how they came to our world: using enormous machines capable of flight!

What follows next is a fragment of the conversation between the beings:

<. . . the hell was that?>

<What was what?>

<That crunching sound. Did you step on something?>

<I don't think . . . oh, man! That's disgusting!>

<Look at that. You crushed the poor thing!>

<It's not my fault it didn't run away.>

<You should be more careful.>

<Why do you care about some random critter? There are probably millions of them on this dump of a planet.>

<How would you feel if someone stepped on you?>

<That's different. I'm smart enough to stay out of the way of something big enough to turn me into a Frittata.>

<How do you know it wasn't intelligent? Maybe it didn't run away because it wanted to say hello.>

<Oh, come on, again with your E. T. theories? Do you really think that if anything even semi-intelligent lived on this planet, they wouldn't

have discovered it yet? You do realize that this sector has been on the map for nearly a century?>

<Maybe they missed the signs . . .>

<Or maybe you should get down to Earth and get it through your head: there are no little green men or super-advanced civilizations. At least not in this Galaxy! We are, and probably always will be all alone.>

<That's not possible. I mean, statistically . . .>

<There are no aliens here! Just let it go, dude, okay? We have a job to do, so let's focus . . .>

[missing passage]

<. . . hey, is this it?>

<Let's see. Blue-slash-turquoise color, soft material . . . yep, that's it.>

<It's open, and . . . take a look at this! Half of that damn thing is literally fused into the ground.>

<Shit! It's like that one three months ago, remember? Ended up right in the middle of that meteorite.>

<True . . . whoever the owner is, they won't be happy. What did they say they had in there?>

<Looks like the regular stuff: clothes, some medicine, personal hygiene stuff, electric razor and . . . heh, this is good: gifts.>

<Gifts? Are you kidding me? We spent two days in that shuttle to bring back cheap crap from a souvenir stand?>

<I don't think these are your run-of-the-mill souvenirs. Check out their listed value.>

<Five grand for a bottle of wine?! Eight for a *hand-crafted wooden statue*?! You're right, this must be some high-end stuff.>

<Yup, and we won't be bringing back any of it which means one thing.>

<Reimbursement. The bosses will be pissed!>

<Hey, it's not our fault. Besides, they should really look into what, exactly, is causing this in the first place. I mean, I know that it's not that common, but what if one day it happens to a passenger? Can you imagine: you're going on vacation or a business trip and all of a sudden, mid-flight, you pop up somewhere else, millions of kilometers away from the ship?>

<That is a disturbing thought. A buddy of mine is an engineer and he once told me that it has to be the Alcubierre. A glitch or a malfunction or something of that sort.>

<That actually makes more sense to me than that bullshit explanation they're feeding us. Seriously, how can they . . .>

This is where the recording ends. Once again, I do realize that much about this discovery remains a mystery but on the other hand, I believe you will agree when I say that the main question of whether or not we are alone in the cosmos has just been sufficiently answered.

Before we move onto your questions, I wish to let you know that the aforementioned items are currently held at my home institute, the Kratiirs Academy of Sciences. I extend an official invitation to not only all of you who are attending the Conference today, but also to your peers to join me and share your invaluable expertise. There is no doubt in my mind that together we can unravel the particularities of this discovery and learn more about our neighbors in the cosmos.

Now, please ask your questions!

09/10/2152   *Private and confidential*

Mr. Jonathan S. Williams

4, Huntington Street

New London

NL12-020

United Europe

EARTH

Our Ref.: 33925281/VR2QNY/NOL

Dear Mr. Williams:

We refer to your online baggage claim dated, 20 September 2152.

We deeply regret to inform you that, despite our best efforts, we were unable to successfully recover your delayed luggage.

Please follow this link to fill out the official reimbursement form by submitting a complete list of all items from your luggage and attaching the receipts. Our Refunds Department will process your claim and contact you within 21 working days.

We sincerely apologize for the inconvenience caused by this unfortunate incident and hope that we can reinstall your trust in our services and standards in the near future.

Yours sincerely,

Frank Azzopardi

Customer Service Department

European Spacelines

Martin Lochman is an emerging author from the Czech Republic, currently living and working as a University librarian in Malta. He first started writing and publishing in Czech but as time went by and his affinity for English language grew, he switched to English. Some of his flash fiction and short stories appeared (or are forthcoming) in Theme of Absence, Asymmetry Fiction, Aphelion, Aurora Wolf, AntipodeanSF, 101Words, The Weird and Whatnot, and 365tomorrows. You can find him at: https://martinlochmanauthor.wordpress.com/ or twitter: @MartinLochman.

KAI HUDSON

DEAD LEGENDS

THE SWEET, FLORAL scent of perfume reaches him before her footsteps do. It's always been this way.

He doesn't move. Her steps are delicate, *tip-tip-tip* with the occasional crunch of the roof's crumbling tile beneath stiletto. He has to give her credit: she doesn't stumble once as she comes up to join him on the roof, a cool presence just over his left shoulder. "Hello, Ashton." He hears the smile in her voice.

Traitorous pleasure stirs at the base of his spine. How many years has it been since they last spoke? However many, it is not enough.

Like him, she goes by many names. Lady Red. Spirit Devil Who Lives in Mist. Silkwoman, in all the headlines. But to him, she has only ever had one name.

"Mariah." It comes out rougher than he means to, and he coughs. *This damned smoke.* "It's been a long time."

"Too long, I'd say." A soft rustle as she sits down next to him, tucking the folds of her dress neatly beneath her thighs. The wind brings a rush of orchid-jasmine-orange; his eyes water with the familiar comfort of it. Or maybe that's just the ash.

He stares at her, because he can't not. She hasn't aged a day, still the exact same woman from almost sixty years ago; it's all there in the thin, girlish nose, the full lips, long wavy hair the color of fallen pine needles. He blinks and sees the beach in Guam stretched out behind her, bright blue ocean glittering a thousand diamonds a minute. The soft brush of her hand over his palm. Her smile, dizzying, solid around her lies, had reeled him in squirming and helpless.

He breaks quickly away. "You look good."

Her hand comes to rest on his arm. The touch is warm and full of gentle promise, but he knows now to focus instead on the long, sharp fingernails, five needles just waiting to pierce. "I'm afraid I can't say the same for you."

There is real sadness there; beneath the *matryoshka* layers of deceit, she loved them all, in her own way. He drops his gaze down to the blanket in his lap, the hard metal frame of the wheelchair digging into his back. He doesn't know what she sees, but he knows what he feels: every one of his ninety-two years. A miracle, really, that he made it this far, but then again, what did Code-11 do besides miracles?

He takes a deep breath—hard with all the smoke, but he manages. "How did you find me?"

"I Googled 'old white guy in Thailand.'"

He manages a laugh, but it quickly fades into another round of coughing. His lungs burn. He's been here for over a month now, waiting for people to recognize him, to spread the rumors, creating just enough vibrations in the web to draw Mariah's attention. But it's been hell on his aging body. He looks back out at the town around them. You can't see the fires here, not yet, but a dull orange glow paints the sky beyond the rolling mountains, and the wind brings the pungent smell of burnt foliage and animal bones. Southeast Asia is on fire.

Kachik! There is a flicker of flame as Mariah lights a cigarette. She never smoked when they were together, said she despised the smell. How people change.

"Is Jasperite with you?" He keeps the question casual, harmless. Nothing to see here, just an old man making desperate conversation.

Mariah shrugs. "He's cleaning up the last of the rebels outside Tel Aviv. You know how it is. Says hi, though."

He clamps down on the disappointment. It was always a long shot, he knew, but Jasperite is the one who started all this, and he had hoped . . . well. He should know better than to hope by now.

Beneath the blanket, his right hand clenches into a fist. At least Mariah is here. At least he gets to have this.

If she senses the slow gathering of energy in his arm, she chooses not to show it, shifting and exhaling a cloud of smoke. "I wish we didn't have to meet again under these circumstances."

"I wish you hadn't killed all my friends and helped a megalomaniac destroy the world, but we can't all have what we want."

"That's not fair." She frowns, reaches for him—his breath catches—but then she just rearranges the blanket over his legs, tucking it tenderly in against his body. Her eyes betray nothing but sadness, and he smothers a smile. Finally, a win: she sees him only the way he wants her to, old and frail. Good. Let her be drawn in by his weak appearance. For all Silkwoman's prowess, she is the one caught in his web now. She'll never see it coming.

"I wish you would come back with me, Bussy." Ash drips from the end of her cigarette. "I wish you would embrace just how special you are."

Special. They use that word to describe

everyone these days, but he remembers back in Guam when it actually meant something. All those years ago when it was just the First Four—him, Shadowling, Tigress, and Berserker—Code-11's first success with full-body irradiation to initiate rapid gene mutation. The first true superheroes. Saviors of the world.

It was pure dumb luck how Code-11's radiation hit him differently. In everyone else it found complete saturation, each gene individually modified to produce Shadowling's eyeblink-fast phasing, Tigress's enhanced senses and super speed, and Berserker's gigantic, lumbering bulk. But for him it concentrated instead, sent its free-radical settlers out to the unexplored frontier of his right arm and established them there in colonies of buzzing, radiant energy. It failed to enslave his whole self, which is the only reason why Mariah paid him so much attention after the procedure. And why, of the First Four, he is the only one still alive.

The grief hits him, fresh even after sixty years. Tigress, with her love of ales so pale they were practically water. Shadowling, whose silly puns always produced more groans than laughter. Berserker, who'd finally admitted one night after three bottles of vodka that he'd always secretly dreamed of joining the Moscow ballet.

Soon, Ashton thinks. He'll be with them very soon.

The dilapidated housing complex across the street is covered in faded posters, identical prints coated in soot so thick he can't distinguish their message. It's hardly necessary: the image is seared into his brain, along with its terrible message.

Code-11: No evil shall stand

Jasperite's motto is plastered on posters all over buildings, inked on pamphlets scattered down from the sky, purred between broadcasts on every radio station across the globe. *No evil shall stand.*

Took Ashton a while to really get it. You can't blame him: Mariah is living proof he's not the best-stitched cape on the rack. Like everyone else, he thought at first it was only meant to be a warning to terrorists and pirates and gun runners: watch your back, this is our turf now.

Decades later, he knows better. *No evil shall stand* isn't a slogan, it's an opioid. Let us take care of it, is what Jasperite means. No matter what wickedness you see or terrors you witness, our superheroes will come and save you eventually. Good will defeat evil; just you wait and see.

The world, as it turns out, is a sucker for the promise of happy endings.

If Jasperite's in Tel Aviv now, the rebels have no chance. Of all the world governments, Israel lasted the longest, held out for an additional twenty years after the fall of Japan before Jasperite's agents finally managed to infiltrate, before the epidemic of passivity finally took hold. Now Tel Aviv is a crumbling ruin, its remaining citizens looking to the sky like everyone else, swapping the heroism inside them for a quavering hope of nonexistent rescue.

This crumbling, cowardly world, where honeybees see the wasps coming and, instead of swarming to their own defense, simply lie still with the desperate delusion that bumblebees with bigger stingers will come save them. But the honeybees don't know their so-called protectors are slaves, and once the wasps decide they are of no further use . . .

He shudders and glances at Mariah. She's letting the silence stretch, probably thinking he's zoned out in dementia and will start drooling any moment now. *Let her assume.* The energy in his hand is building to true heat now, glowing embers just waiting to light. He only needs to keep her here a couple minutes longer, and then . . .

Then he'll avenge them all. Shadowling, Tigress, Berserker, and everyone else Code-11 produced, then enslaved, brainwashed, and ultimately murdered once the world's population was subdued into complacency. The radiation suffusing every cell in his friends' bodies made it easy: flip a switch and *voila,* catastrophic organ failure. But Ashton is different. Code-11 only owned his arm, and yes, they took that from him. But not, as it turns out, for good. Tonight, he's back. Tonight, he will give them something to fear.

The building heat in the air finally catches Mariah's attention. The cigarette pauses halfway to her lips, and her eyes go wide. "Ashton?"

The way she says it—startled, uncertain, scared—sparks sudden rage. Where was this vulnerability when his friends died? Where was it when every government toppled, one after the other, its citizens poisoned to their very bones by Jasperite's cocktail of security? Where was it when she used him, *abused* him, all so her boss could keep him out of the way as he established cold dominion over the world?

Lightning gathers in his right fist, and beneath the blanket, a faint blue light begins to glow. The power sings, reaches out to him just the way it used to, the way it hasn't in decades. It's a miracle, exactly how that Resistance doctor described it when she came to him a few months ago with the injections, her voice humming with excitement as she spoke fancy terms like *isotopic*

resurge and *gamma-ionic reradiation.* He only really heard one thing—*you'll get it back*—and now that it's here he wants to cry with how much he's missed it, but mostly he wants to *kill.* Annihilate Mariah and Jasperite and all of Code-11 in one blast. Save the world just like he used to.

Be a hero again.

Mariah straightens as blue light permeates the air. She doesn't run, doesn't do anything, even as he bares his teeth and lifts his arm from beneath the blanket. There it is: the pattern of veins bulging just beneath his skin, glowing a bright, luminescent blue with pent-up energy just waiting to be released. Revenge at last. Finally, he will set the world right.

He aims his fist at her. "My name," he snarls, "is Blunderbuss."

If this were that kind of story, he would fire. An energy blast the size of a large boulder would shoot from his fist, obliterating Silkwoman even before she could scream. And then it would continue on to the street below where (because she lies) Jasperite waits with a crew of commandos, and the blast would take them as well—blow them into bits and leave nothing but a smoking crater in the earth. And from that initial blast Blunderbuss would throw off his pretext of weakness, would leap from the roof and down onto the street without a care. He would head back into the woods to find the Resistance and lead them to glorious victory not a year later, relegating Code-11 to nothing but a dark blip in the history books. It would be wonderful, and so very right. Good defeating evil, just the way it's supposed to be.

How happy does that make you, my little honeybee?

A wave of dizziness hits him, vertigo and

nausea sapping his strength in one quick instant. Ashton moans and collapses back into the wheelchair. His arm flops atop the blanket, the blue veins pulsing once before fading to nothing. The power dissipates as easy as the smoke still wafting up from Mariah's cigarette.

The world spins around him. He gasps for breath, sweat running down his face, all his limbs suddenly turned to stone. What's going on?

Silkwoman grins, showing sharp teeth. "Dr. Phuong was so very enthusiastic, wasn't she?" she says.

Ashton stares. Mariah lifts her free hand and draws a nameless shape in the air. Her fingers leave shimmering silken threads, and as smoke and ash continue to float down from the sky, the gossamer strands gather together, forming a familiar face, the same face that smiled warmly at Ashton during all those previous visits as she bent over his arm and inserted the needle . . .

"No."

He's barely aware that he said it aloud, staring in horror as the Resistance doctor— his last hope, his last glimmer of light in this burning world—fades into nothing with a wave of Mariah's hand. Silkwoman's smile widens, her teeth pale bones in the dark. "You never thought to ask what was in her injections, did you? Poor Ashton. Always so gullible."

The cigarette goes out. Mariah rises and mashes it to nothing beneath her shoe. Her eyes glint in the half-light, and what he sees there makes him shudder and try to run, but now even that is too much: his body turned to stone, his last ally betrayed.

"The paralysis is permanent. If you don't starve to death first, the fires'll find you eventually." Mariah saunters up to him and plants a hand on each arm of the wheelchair. Her perfume brings a fresh wave of nausea, but he can't move away, can barely even blink. She leans closer, lips brushing his ear in a soft, venomous kiss.

"Long live the Resistance."

He moans, pitiful. Silkwoman's fanged smile floats away into the dark. Blunderbuss, last of the Four, flops limply in his wheelchair, mouth forming shapeless words snatched up by the wind.

Beyond the mountains the jungle fires continue to burn, ruthless with finality.

Kai Hudson lives in sunny California where she writes, hikes, and spends entirely too much time daydreaming of far-off worlds. Her work has appeared in Clarkesworld, PseudoPod, PodCastle, Anathema: Spec from the Margins, and other fine places. Find her at kaihudson.com.

THE DAY AFTER CHARLIE MOTLEY DIED

ALEX DE-GRUCHY

I CARRIED A revolver, a rifle, a knife and a crucifix, and while I only really believed in the stopping power of three of those things, I knew it didn't hurt to carry the fourth.

The world was a strange place, after all. Take my temporary travelling companion: a man having a rough day partly because he was hungover and partly because he was dead. "Gimme some water," Motley rasped.

"I told you a half-dozen times already," I said, "you're dead, you don't need water anymore. Your brain's just playing tricks on you."

"Quit saying that, you son of a bitch! I ain't dead! Do I sound like a dead man to you? Huh?"

I sighed and pulled my Paint to a halt. It was hot and although I hadn't yet known Motley a day, I'd already had enough of his bellyaching. The mustang on which he sat, with his hands tied together behind his back, stopped as it neared my own mount. I adjusted my hat and swung down from my saddle. I held a length of rope, one end in my hand and the other secured to the neck of the mustang, and now I tied my end to the horn of my saddle.

I walked over to Motley, the soles of my boots crunching on the loose rock of the gentle slope we'd been climbing. He eyed me suspiciously as I approached, shifting in his saddle and licking his dry lips. I reached up with both hands, grabbed him by the front of his shirt, and yanked. He didn't have time to protest as I turned him so that he landed on his back, and in seconds I had a knee on his stomach and a hand on one of his shoulders, pinning him down.

Motley kicked and squirmed. I drew my Bowie knife from its sheath on my hip and held it up in front of his face, making sure he saw it very clearly.

"No, no, no–" Motley's voice rose alongside his mounting panic, his eyes fixed on the long blade. I didn't consider myself a cruel man, so I didn't wait too long before slamming the knife down into his chest, the blade piercing his shirt and sliding between his ribs almost all the way up to the guard.

Motley began to scream but I was in no mood for it. Besides, we were in wild country and I didn't want to draw any unnecessary attention, so I took my right hand from my knife and clamped it over his mouth. His eyes bulged as he stared at the knife buried in his chest, his screaming mercifully muffled now.

"Motley," I said.

But he wasn't listening. Instead he just went on screaming into my hand, his patchy beard rubbing unpleasantly against my palm.

"*Look at me, Motley*," I demanded, and this time his eyes met mine. "You feel that knife in your chest?"

Motley looked at my knife, blinked, frowned as he gave it some thought, and then looked back at me. He shook his head.

"That's right," I nodded. "You see any blood pouring outta your chest?"

Another look at the knife, another shake of the head.

"Now this is the last time I'm gonna lay this out for you," I said. "You're not feeling any pain because you're *dead*. Understand? Tomorrow you'll be nothing but dust and bones, but for now you've got one day left on this Earth and I intend for you to make

yourself useful in that time. So, you're gonna quit your whining and we're gonna ride along together a little while longer. Just a few more hours until we get where we need to be. Then, once you've done your part, I'll give you a reward. You name it. Within reason. You have my word."

Motley stared at me, confused and breathing hard. "Do we have a deal?" I asked.

Even an intelligent man would've had a hard time swallowing what I'd just said, and Motley was not an intelligent man. But to his credit, he seemed to accept the truth as well as a man in his rare situation could, and nodded slowly.

"Alright," I said. "Now, I'm gonna take my hand off your mouth and my knife outta your chest. No more screaming."

I took hold of my knife and pulled it free, the blade sliding out smoothly. There was congealed blood on it, and I wiped it off on Motley's shirt before returning the knife to its sheath. He looked down at the dark stain and then up at me with an indignant frown. "Hey, you don't need to make a bigger mess of my shirt."

I took my knee off Motley's stomach and rose to my feet, grabbing one of his upper arms and pulling him up with me. I helped him back up onto his saddle, the horse to which it was attached snorting and flicking its ears, sensing the unnatural nature of its rider. I stroked its neck a few times and muttered, "Easy."

Motley was staring down at his chest. "So I'm really dead, huh?" he said.

"Yeah."

He looked off across the rocky hills stretching into the distance, his eyes narrowed as he squinted against the bright midday sunlight, his mouth open slightly. "Well, shit," he said finally.

I left Charlie Motley—outlaw in life and philosopher in death—to his thoughts as I untied the rope from my saddle horn, holding it in one hand again, and climbed back up onto my Paint. I gave the horse my spurs and we continued onwards, a talking dead man at my back and far stranger things ahead.

Motley stopped asking for water, but he didn't stop with the questions.

He asked who I was. I told him he could call me "Corwin."

He asked what I did for a living. I told him I did a bunch of things.

He asked how he'd died, because he didn't remember. I told him he'd passed out drunk in a bath and drowned. When the whore he'd hired for the night found him, she told her boss, who then had Motley's corpse dressed, carried out of his saloon, and tossed into a ditch at the edge of town. That was where I found him and brought him back to life— of a kind—and it was during this process that I'd been able to learn the circumstances of his death.

He asked if I was the Devil. I told him I wasn't but that I'd heard the Devil did visit these parts from time to time.

He asked what made him so special. I told him not a thing. I just needed a dead man, and Lady Luck had been forthcoming enough to run a hand up my thigh and have me stumble across Motley's fresh corpse lying at the edge of the lawless, piss- and blood-soaked back-water that was the town of Dahlia.

Eventually I told Motley question time was over. It was late afternoon now and although the sun still beat down, we were at least out of the worst of it thanks to the vast expanse of woodland through which we rode,

the sunlight only breaking through where the crowding foliage overhead allowed it to.

We were high up in the hills, the pine trees growing thick and wild here, the forest floor carpeted with fallen green needles which made gentle crunching sounds beneath our horses' hooves.

The horses were nervous, their snorting and heavy breathing loud in the hushed still-ness of the forest. No wind rustled the trees or bushes, and apart from occasional, distant birdcalls, I hadn't heard or seen any signs of animal life in nearly an hour. It wasn't unusual to catch sight of deer or bighorn sheep in the lower hills, but up here not even a prairie dog or fox squirrel crossed our path. Unlike me, the animals were smart enough to keep away from this place. But then, they didn't have to worry about keeping promises.

"I got an itch," Motley said from behind me, my hand still gripping the rope which pulled his mount on.

"Shut up," I said.

"Come on, Corwin, it's a bad one. You know when you get one right between your balls and your leg? I can't get to it with my hands tied. I'm not gonna run, not all the way out here. Can't you untie me already?"

I looked back at Motley. "*Shut. Up.*"

Motley opened his mouth to say some-thing when an arrow suddenly buried itself in his chest. Whatever words he'd intended to speak were replaced with a surprised gasp.

I was a little surprised myself. Although I'd expected that goddamn Cheyenne to get the drop on us however alert I might be, I didn't expect him to announce his presence in quite so dramatic a fashion.

Motley's eyes were wide as he stared down at the arrow. "Oh, Jesus!"

"Remember what I said about the screaming," I reminded him as I turned my head back around and pulled my Paint to a halt, the mustang stopping in turn.

The Cheyenne was there, of course, right before my eyes and less than thirty feet away. I'd only looked back at Motley for a second, but it had been long enough for the Cheyenne to slip out from where he'd been watching us—hidden right in our path—and put an arrow in the dead man's chest.

I nodded at the dark eyes that stared back at mine. "Blood River."

The Cheyenne lowered his bow and I watched him as he approached, my nerves on edge. He wasn't my enemy, but anyone with a lick of sense would recognize Blood River as a man to be careful around. Hell, the name was a clue.

He came to a stop a few feet away, his bow slung over his shoulder now. Along with the bow he carried a tomahawk, a revolver, and a rifle. He wore moccasins, breechcloths, and leather leggings but nothing over his torso, so the numerous scars on his chest and back were plain to see. His long, black braids framed a lined face and eyes which had clearly seen much, little of it good.

Although he carried a dog rope, Blood River's days as a Dog Soldier were over, if he'd ever been one at all. I barely knew the man but I knew he had no tribe, no family, no brothers-in-arms. Whatever he might've been in the past, he was a loner now. As for me, I was as alone as any haunted man could be.

"Was that really necessary?" I asked.

Blood River glanced at Motley. "I wanted to see if he was what you promised."

"As you can see, he is. And if he *wasn't* dead before, he sure would be now."

"It ain't right, treating me like this!"

Motley called out. "You say I'm dead, then you stab me, then a damn redskin shoots me with an arrow! It ain't right, Corwin, you hear me?"

Blood River's expression didn't change as he looked at me and said, "He doesn't need his tongue to serve our purpose."

I looked back at Motley. "You hear that? This *redskin* wants to cut your tongue out, and I'm not gonna get in his way if he decides to do it. You don't want that to happen. I suggest you take the advice I've been trying to give you and shut the hell up."

Motley looked down at the ground with a sulky frown and mumbled, "It ain't right."

I turned back to Blood River. "He'll do as he's told. You been keeping an eye on the lothurms?"

"I watched them for a time before dawn. There was no change in their pattern."

"Then they should be asleep for the next few hours, and Charlie here can get in and out before they wake up."

"What're you guys talking about?" asked Motley. "What's a . . . *lothurm*?"

I thought about what Motley would soon come face-to-face with and almost felt sorry for him. "I'll explain along the way."

Of course Motley didn't believe me until he saw the things for himself, and when he did he would've screamed if I hadn't been ready for it and clamped my hand over his mouth again. I wasn't annoyed this time: screaming the first time you see a lothurm is an understandable reaction.

"Quiet," I whispered to Motley. He nodded as if in a daze, his eyes never leaving the lothurms. I took my hand away from his mouth, which hung open as he stared.

Blood River was staring at the lothurms as well, but his face might as well have been carved from stone for all you could tell from it.

Motley, Blood River, and I were lying on our bellies in the dirt on the crest of a small hill, the slope before us gradually leading down to a cave mouth about eighty to ninety feet away. Blood River had plucked his arrow from Motley's chest and I'd removed the length of rope I used to bind his wrists.

Here the woods were even thicker than before, enough that you were lucky to catch even a glimpse of blue through the trees. And still that unnatural silence. We were in the dark heart of the forest now. We'd left the horses tied up a couple of miles back and walked the rest of the way; this place would've spooked them too badly.

The lothurms were sprawled in the dirt at the mouth of the cave. There were four of them, each as big as a cow, and they were asleep, their sickly-gray torsos rising and falling as they breathed, their tiny eyes closed, pale fluid dribbling from the puckered orifices which served as their mouths. Their snouts and tentacles twitched occasionally as if they were dreaming, although I had no idea what such abominations could be dreaming about.

Bones were strewn around the lothurms and more could be seen just inside the cave, before its interior was claimed by darkness. Most of the bones belonged to animals but there were human ones, too. And there was other evidence of human victims: torn and blood-stained clothing, a bedroll, a rifle.

The railroads, the cattle barons, civilization in general were all in such a rush to expand and push into every corner of this country, never stopping to think that maybe some corners were best avoided, that maybe what

they saw as their God-given right to claim land as their own might not really be worth a damn in some places.

"He goes in now," Blood River said.

He was right. The lothurms were asleep now but the sun was already beginning to set and they'd wake when night fell. The longer we lingered, the more danger we were putting ourselves in. It was time for Motley to make himself useful.

Although, he looked about as useful as a nun in a whorehouse at that moment, still staring slack-jawed as he was. I nudged him with an elbow. "Hey."

That startled him, and he turned to face me. He shook his head. "Those things can't be real."

"I know it's been a day of surprises for you, Charlie, but I need you to focus. Remember what I told you on the way here?"

The lothurms had a voracious appetite for warm, vital flesh and blood but no interest in dead flesh, and that's what Motley was now. If Blood River and I went into the lothurms' lair, we'd be torn apart, but Motley could waltz in there with no trouble at all.

That was my theory, anyway. Although I'd left out the "theory" part when telling Motley all this.

I'd told Motley about the lothurms' hunger for living flesh, about how they usually lived together in small groups and were never seen out in the open or near civilization, instead sticking to deep woodland. No one knew what they were or where they'd come from, but they'd been around a long time if Blood River was right: I'd heard stories about lothurms, but Blood River had heard legends.

And it was this particular group of lothurms which the Cheyenne and I were interested in, and which would allow me to pay off the debt

I'd owed Blood River for the past ten months, ever since one storm-wracked afternoon at Lowell's Rock when he stopped a witch from claiming my soul. He hadn't helped me out of friendship, but it was a debt I needed to clear.

In the lair of these sleeping lothurms was an item which Blood River wanted but couldn't retrieve himself, due to the danger. I doubted he was scared of anything in this world, but that didn't mean he was stupid. So why not get the white man who owed him a favor to do the dirty work for him?

And that's what had led to me binding Charlie Motley's soul to his body for a time after his natural death: like Blood River, why shouldn't I get someone else to do my dirty work for me? Sorry, Charlie, but shit rolls downhill.

Once I'd repaid my debt to Blood River, I'd do what needed to be done next. Although I was determined to do the former, I still wasn't so sure about the latter, but doubt was a luxury I could only afford for so long.

"But *look* at those things!" Motley hissed. "I'm not going down there!"

"We've been through this. Believe me, they've got no interest in you. This is why I brought you back to life. All the effort I've gone to today, you think I'd've done all that just to feed you to these things now?"

"Christ, I don't know! I've had a knife *and* an arrow in my heart today and I'm still sucking air, what the hell am I supposed to think anymore?"

"No more waiting," Blood River said.

I gripped Motley's nearest shoulder. "Listen to me. You still have some time left on this Earth thanks to me, but I could take that away right now. Do you remember what happened after you died?"

"No."

"And do you know why that is? It's because there *is* nothing after you die. No Heaven, no Hell, nothing. Same as how it was before you were born, just an absence of everything. *Forever.* That's what you've got coming. It's what we've *all* got coming. But right here, right now, you're still among the living, and if you wanna hang onto that any longer, you'll do what I said. Forever is a long time, Charlie."

Motley rubbed his jaw with one hand. He looked at the lothurms then back at me.

"You already know you don't feel pain anymore," I said. "You've got nothing to be afraid of."

"A metal box," Motley said.

"That's right. Black, with a silver lock. It's in that cave, and all we need is for you to fetch it."

"What's in it?"

"I told you, you don't need to worry about that. You just need to bring it to us."

Motley scratched his head and frowned. Here was a man who never used his brain much beyond deciding what to drink, poke, steal or kill next, but even stupid men want to survive, even if only for a little longer. Men who were truly prepared to die were few and far between when it came right down to it.

Motley nodded. "Alright."

"Good. It's just those four lothurms, and the cave doesn't go back that far. Tread carefully: they won't hurt you if you wake them up, but if they keep sleeping then all the better."

Motley looked down the slope at the sleeping, twitching creatures. "Alright," he repeated. He carefully got to his feet and began creeping towards the mouth of the cave.

Blood River and I watched him as he went, Motley holding his hands out slightly at his sides as if trying to balance on a beam, daintily tip-toeing in a futile attempt to reduce the noise his footsteps made. He obviously hadn't had much practice when it came to stealth, and if he looked like an idiot to my eyes then I hated to think what Blood River—a man who could be as quiet as a shadow—made of him.

"He is a fool," Blood River said. That answered that question.

"But a useful one in his condition," I said. "I told you I'd find a way to get you that cash-box."

Motley slowed as he approached the lothurms and then stopped completely as one of them grunted and briefly thrashed a tentacle in its sleep, sending up a small spray of earth and pine needles. Motley looked back at us and even from this distance I could see the fear on his face.

Don't panic, you son of a bitch, I thought. If he did and drew those lothurms to us then we'd be in real trouble, especially with our horses miles away. My rifle was at my side, one hand resting on it. My grip on it tightened.

But Motley didn't panic. Instead he turned back to the task at hand, resuming his walk towards the cave and creeping around the sleeping lothurms. He paused at the threshold of the cave, looked around, and then went inside. He was quickly swallowed by the darkness.

Blood River spotted Motley before I did. "He's coming," he said.

I squinted, peering into the dark cave interior, but it was still a couple of seconds before I made out what Blood River had already seen: Charlie Motley, carrying a metal box in both hands, stepping warily towards the daylight.

I couldn't help but smile when I saw he was wearing a hat which hadn't been on his head when he'd entered the cave. As well as collecting the cash-box for us, he'd apparently helped himself to something while he was there. Once a thief. . . .

Motley slowly made his way out of the cave and past the lothurms, all of which were still sleeping. Once he'd put a little distance between himself and them, he quickened his pace, frequently looking back over his shoulder as he ascended the slope towards us. Blood River and I crouch-walked back a few feet, enough so that we were out of sight of the lothurms. Each of us held his rifle in his hands. We rose to our full height just as Motley crested the slope.

He walked towards us on unsteady legs, his chest rising and falling even though he didn't need to breathe anymore. Hard to kick a habit like that, I guess.

Blood River slung his rifle over one shoulder and took the cash-box from Motley.

The outlaw frowned at the Cheyenne. "You're *welcome.*"

I nodded at Motley's new headwear. "Nice hat."

Motley looked up at the hat as he adjusted the brim with both hands. It *was* a nice hat. And it was black, so you could hardly make out the soaked-in bloodstains.

"It was just sitting there," Motley said. " Bastard saloon-owner back in Dahlia must've kept my old hat. You should've seen some of the stuff in that cave, all kinds of shit."

I turned to Blood River, who'd already started walking back in the direction of our horses.

"Come on," I said to Motley, and we followed the Cheyenne through silent woods that were getting darker by the minute and in which the lothurms would soon hunt.

We came to a stop near our horses, which remained tied to the trunk of the thick pine where we'd left them, occasionally tugging at their bonds. There were miles between us and the lothurms now and the forest was less overwhelming here, but being able to see more of the sky didn't help all that much when it was already turning black and filling with stars. These hills, these woods, this whole damn business with Blood River: I just wanted to put it all behind me.

Blood River got down onto his knees, placed the metal cash-box on the ground and began to work the lid with the head of his tomahawk in an attempt to pry it open. He hadn't said a word since Motley had exited the cave.

"I recognize a cash-box when I see it, y'know," Motley said. "You didn't tell me it was money you were after."

I ignored him, my attention focused on Blood River.

Eventually the lid popped open and Blood River put his tomahawk back in its place on his hip. Motley and I looked at the contents of the cash-box: hundreds of crumpled five-dollar bills, all shoved carelessly inside.

Motley gave an impressed whistle.

Blood River was staring at the cash. "Is that it?" I asked him.

He reached into the cash-box and grabbed two handfuls of bills then held them up and closed his eyes. He chanted a few things in Cheyenne—I recognized some of the words but most were lost on me—and then fell silent again. When he opened his eyes, they were covered in a milky-white film. He blinked and it vanished.

"Jesus," Motley muttered as he grimaced and took a step backwards.

"It is," Blood River said.

I reached a hand into one of the interior pockets of my duster, my other hand holding my rifle down at my side. "Here," I said to Blood River as I withdrew a match and tossed it to him. He opened one hand, dropping the cash it held back into the cash-box, and caught the match. He placed the other handful of money back in the cash-box as well. He struck the match, his body bathed in the orange glow of the small flame.

"Hey, hold on now," Motley said.

Blood River dropped the match into the cash-box.

"*What the hell are you doing?!*" Motley cried out with genuine outrage and horror in his voice as the money began to blacken and burn. Neither Blood River nor I answered him. The Cheyenne was watching the money and I was watching the Cheyenne.

We stood like that until the small fire died down and the cash-box contained nothing but ashes and embers. Motley shook his head. "Now that there's a damn shame," he said sadly.

There was silence then until Blood River looked up at me and said, "The curse is lifted."

And that was when I raised my rifle and shot him in the head.

"*Jesus Christ!*" Motley said as the kneeling Blood River tipped over, blood spraying from the large hole in the back of his head, pieces of skull and brain scattered across the earth and grass behind him. He hit the ground, twitched a couple of times, then lay still. I watched him for a few seconds before finally lowering my rifle.

The shot had been uncomfortably loud in the stillness, my mind immediately conjuring the image of four lothurms hurriedly shambling through the forest towards the source of the noise.

ALEX DE-GRUCHY '16

"I thought you were friends!" Motley said, his eyes moving between Blood River and me.

"No," I said. "We just weren't enemies. I owed him a debt and I paid it."

"And then you blew his damn head off! And what the hell was the point of me going through those goddamn monsters to fetch that money if you were just gonna burn it?"

"The money in that cash-box was cursed. There was Cheyenne blood on it, the blood of people this man used to know. He'd been looking for it a long time. He needed to burn it with his own hands to lift the curse and set free the spirits of those who died because of that money. When he found out where the cash-box was, he called in the debt I owed him."

"Sounds like some mumbo-jumbo bullshit to me," Motley said.

Said the dead man, I thought. I stared at the embers in the cash-box. They were just a few tiny, fading pinpricks of orange light now. "It's what he believed."

I holstered my rifle and walked over to Blood River's horse. I untied it and slapped it on the rump, and it ran off through the trees. I silently wished it luck.

Motley took another swig from the whiskey bottle and swallowed. After a moment he frowned and began working his tongue around inside his mouth. Then he opened wide and reached a dirty thumb and forefinger inside. They came back out holding a rotten tooth. Motley studied it for a moment, turning it this way and that, before finally flicking it away. He looked pale and drawn in the dawn light. It wouldn't be long now.

"Why'd you kill that Indian?" Motley asked.

"Why do you care?" I said.

He shrugged. "Just wondering."

We were sitting on a hill overlooking a valley through which a narrow river ran, far away now from the lothurms and the forest that was their home. A cloudless sky stretched for miles, the breeze was cool on the skin, and the grass was thick and green. You could hear the calls of birds as they darted across the sky or perched in trees, and although the river was far below us, the steady sound of its rushing waters carried on the air. As the final view before you died, it beat a whore's tin bath or the inside of a lothurm's mouth.

Our horses were tethered to a tree just up the hill, within sight but far enough away from Motley that his presence didn't make

them nervous. I looked over at the whiskey bottle which dangled in one of Motley's hands, but then thought better of it. He'd almost finished it, might as well let him have the rest. It wasn't much of a reward for his help, but it had been the best I could do. And in truth, Motley seemed happy enough with it.

"I killed Blood River because if I didn't then he was gonna do something very bad in the future," I said. "A massacre. I had the chance to stop it, so I took it. *After* I'd cleared my debt."

"How'd you know he was gonna do that?" Motley asked. "He tell you?"

"In case you didn't notice, he wasn't much of a talker. A ghost told me."

Motley chewed on that in silence for a moment before taking another swallow of whiskey.

"But you said when you die, there ain't anything afterwards," Motley said. "So how come you talked to a ghost?"

"Because being a ghost isn't really life after death. A ghost is more like a photograph of someone that used to be alive, a faded copy that lingers even after that person's dead. Still, some of them, sometimes, can know things. About the past, the present . . . and the future."

Motley coughed a deep, rattling cough. He cleared his throat and spat. "So, who's the ghost who told you what the Indian was gonna do?"

"Someone I used to know."

Motley shook his head and smiled then took another drink. I guess he'd heard and seen enough crazy bullshit for one day. He had his new hat and his whiskey, and that would do.

We sat in silence for a time. The sun was rising, brightening the landscape and warming the day. Eventually I heard the thump of the whiskey bottle hitting the ground. I looked over at it. It was empty.

Motley's head and shoulders were slumped forward, his forearms resting on his knees, his hands dangling. His hat had been pushed to an untidy angle. I adjusted it for him.

I stood up, brushed the grass and dirt off the backside of my duster, and began walking towards the horses.

It was the scent I noticed first. It always was. That clean, slightly sweet smell which had always clung to her after she came out of the bath.

Then she was walking beside me. I didn't look directly at her, but out of the corner of my eye I could see how the breeze blew her hair around her face and rustled her dress.

I reminded myself that the breeze was doing no such thing. Because there *was* no hair there, no dress, nothing.

"A faded copy?" she said. "Is that what I am to you?"

She might not have been real, but the faint stab I felt in my gut at the sound of her voice, that was real enough. Every damn time.

I kept my eyes on the horses, kept walking.

"You did the right thing," she said. "Killing Blood River saved a lot of innocent people."

"Or maybe I killed an innocent man," I said, immediately recognizing it as a stupid thing to say. Blood River was no more innocent than I was.

"I never lied to you when I was alive, why would I start now? Besides, in the end you still trusted me enough to pull the trigger."

I stopped. She did the same.

"That's right," I said. "I did. And if you're what you claim to be then I got no regrets. On the other hand, maybe I'm crazy and you're just in my head, or maybe you're the Devil himself leading me down a darker path than the one I was already on. Whatever the case, you're not Claudia. Claudia's dead and gone."

I forced myself to look at her. There was nothing there. I stood on the hill, as alone as any haunted man could be.

Alex De-Gruchy is a writer of fiction and non-fiction whose work has covered comic books, radio, video games, prose, and more. You can find him on Twitter at: @AlexDeGruchy.

DREW NORTON

PSYCHIC SAM, P.I.

SAM SLOUCHED BEHIND his battered desk. He took a slug of single malt, lit a hand-rolled cigarette, and opened a newspaper.

"Yeah, Betty, send her in," Sam called through the door before any knock came.

A blonde walked in. "Nice to meet you. I'm—"

"It was the Mob," Sam said. "They killed your husband. Your man discovered the mayor's gang ties and deviant sexual proclivities, then tried blackmailing him. Pretty stupid."

"Oh," she said, slightly flustered. "Should I—"

"Yeah, leave town. Give Betty a hundred bucks for my fee and she'll get you settled."

"Thanks." The woman left.

Sam's gaze never left the newspaper.

———————

Drew Norton is a writer living in the Emerald City of Eugene, OR. He lives with his fiancée, Katie, and a fat cat named Nasu. He was recently published in Wild Musette Journal.

J. D. BLOOD

Vamp in A

"HEY KID. WANNA donate blood?"

He sat behind the counter at what appeared to be a lemonade stand, except there was no lemonade and instead of being on some child's grassy lawn it was wedged between two buildings on an empty city street. He was totally within the shadow of an oversized umbrella: pale face and beady black eyes poked out from under that strange veil of darkness in the otherwise sun-bleached summer afternoon. He was completely motionless, expressionless. He was just . . . *staring.* Long I stood there in the heat—sun beating down like lead, intensely beaming its shimmering waves unto the simmering asphalt—thinking what response I should give to this unusual request.

I looked at him. He looked at me.

Here I noticed two sharp objects protruding from his upper jaw; they rested ever-so-gently on his lower lip, making little indentations where they pressed against his skin. Yep. Those were fangs. At this particular observation, my mind became *quite* made-up:

"Yeah, no thanks."

J. D. Blood is a young author from Long Island, New York who wishes he could simultaneously run off into the woods and make it in the big city. His work appears in Argot Magazine as well as in The Weird and Whatnot. Other than writing, J. D.'s daily activities include studying mathematics, playing music, and relentlessly daydreaming up a world that he someday hopes to put into words. He is allergic to phone calls, but you might be able to track him down if you have a space ship that can time travel and jump between dimensions. Or visit him on Twitter @JDBlood. Whatever works.

MARGARET KARMAZIN

The Top of the Food Chain

THE SHIP SLID silently out of dock and into space. On board, the only living biological entities were Vandermeer, lab rats, bacteria/virus/flora experiments that various scientists had greased palms to get on, a few house-plants, and what was left of me—my original mind. As for Vandemeer, I could download myself into a nanobody once or twice a day to hold and stroke him. A nanobot-constructed body had almost super senses so it would be delicious to cuddle and feel his loud purr.

Harper's reaction when I demanded that my cat come along was predictable.

"No pets. You may construct one from the nanobots whenever you—"

I put my face six centimeters from his. "The cat goes with me."

In space, I was like God if, as some mystics pro-claimed, God is a Mind that creates dream entities within Himself to interact with each other. On a small scale, would I not be doing the same?

As I soared along, I forgot about being small and became All-That-Is . . . at least until I might run into someone else out there.

Was there someone out there?

Mars did have artifacts. Eons ago, people of some type were there, but where were they now? The endless UFO sightings continued as always, elusive and forever just out of reach. Were any of the ancient alien stories true? Just pondering this made me feel a bit glum. Was there nothing to aspire to, nothing beyond us so-dangerously-bumbling humans?

The moment I reached Phobos station, I came to a decision; though Space-Jumps had only been attempted with robot probes, I decided to attempt one even if Spacelab wouldn't approve. It was either that or spend years in a void. "A Jump is what you try after a lot of good, solid exploration," they'd told me. "We don't want to blow this whole thing."

Well, I may be somewhat indestructible now, but I still possessed a mind that could grow weary of the same old, same old.

This method of travel involved Lazar's Sheet. In this scenario, one sees the universe as a flexible sheet on a grid. Place the ship at a certain point on this grid with its gravity generators geared to focus. Choose a point on the flexible sheet where you want the ship to go, direct the ship's generator to focus on that destination, and this will pull the destination point to the ship. Shut off the ship's engine and the ship automatically follows the "stretched fabric" to its goal. No real travel through space; instead the ship bends the fabric of time and space and follows as it springs back, putting you outside the speed of light limit, and when you arrive at the chosen point, you're not a second older. No human consciousness had yet tried the Jump, and possibly it was suicidal.

I transmitted to Phobos Station master, Louis Payne, "Hey, Lou, it's me, Jillian Stone—even though it's not exactly me anymore. Guess what, it's rubber sheet time!" knowing that Lou (and everyone else on the station) would wax hysterical. But I'd itched for this since Matheson worked up his first model of Lazar's wild theory about how UFOs traveled from distant stars, then later when that second robot probe sent back one feeble subspace signal from twenty-three light years away, never to be heard from again.

For whimsical reasons, I chose as my destination Sirius C, the story source of ancient astronauts who taught the rudiments of civilization to humans in Africa, South America, and the Middle East.

"Sirius," I told Lou.

"If you insist on ruining the program, Stone, wouldn't Alpha Centauri be a better choice?"

"Can't make me," I shot back in a totally unprofessional manner. "Aim your earphones toward Sirius C. You might hear from me!"

It felt like nothing at all, not even a pebble rolling off a shelf. Vandermeer did not hesitate a moment in his watch over the lab rats. In a blink, we were 8.611 light years from earth.

Below me was a planet and it was populated.

My send off from Moon Base had been low key and consisted of a small party on board, which I attended in the form of a Bengal tiger just for the hell of it. The old guard who once commanded and manned the space stations wished me well and all that, but I knew they were just relieved that some other sucker took on the job and they were mainly thinking about getting the party over with and moving on to retirement. They left, I left, and sooner than I anticipated, I was heading alone into the starry blackness of the universe.

Immediately, I felt a loneliness that no human could imagine, though as I streamlined toward Mars, I also experienced a sense of wild freedom and escape from the oppression of billions of people. From childhood, I had never been especially fond of my fellow humans.

It began with an overbearing and intrusive mother who had a penchant for stealing my boyfriends. My best friend betrayed me when she "accidentally" messaged to the world my intimate revelations. My bio-father was a serial cheater and drug addict. I was not popular at Cornell—top of my class but socially inept. I tried that outdated institution, marriage, but it only lasted six months. Maybe part of the problem is that I'm 28.653 percent autistic?

Who else did they have for this job that would turn out to be different from what I originally imagined anyway? All of the superior space officers now enjoyed cushy jobs in universities or politics; the last thing they'd desire was to give up their luxurious lives as they were. I remained the best choice. Who else had my particular survival skills, who else had endured the now defunct Starlab Outpost at Neptune for four years with only simulations and messages for company? I thought this would be a long, lonely command, but the usual type of one: like manning a station or ship. But I have to admit I was floored when Harper Knight explained the *real* situation.

"This is no Starlab, Jillian. This deal is pretty much permanent. Certainly, the vessel will be state-of-the-art, the network our best. The hull is memory metal and will repair itself."

"I want the job," I said.

I enjoyed looking at Harper. A perfectly designed android, he was a sight for horny eyes. Two meters tall, wide shoulders tapering to a lean waist, thick black hair, penetrating eyes. "Want to exchange body fluids?" I ventured.

He ignored me and persisted with his original question. "Why do you want the job, Jillian?"

"I worry," I said, "that the human race is finished. At the end of its evolution. Where else can we go beyond the top of the food chain? Everything else is downhill, right? Even our future forays onto asteroids and planets—isn't it all just the same? Conquer the elements, multiply and pollute? I simply want to float in space alone. And yet, I have that deep and lonely wish that *someone* else is out there, that all our battles have not been won."

Harper's expression was, as usual, inscrutable. "This voyage will involve an *irreversible* step, Jillian. There is a bit more to this than I mentioned when we spoke last week. The personality of the individual who takes this voyage will be downloaded into the ship itself. *You will be vacating your body.* The ship itself will become who and what you are."

Even at the age of seventy-two, I could be shocked. My knees buckled and I fell into a chair. "That's quite a bit of information to have left out of last week's conversation."

The planet below me was slightly larger than Earth and was orbiting a red dwarf, apparently Sirius C. Giant Sirius A was intensely visible to my right. Was this planet the source of that Dogon tribal tale of ancient astronauts? They claimed to have been visited and instructed by semi-amphibious beings from a third Sirius star.

I was bombarded with millions of signals. My temporary panic caused the lighting inside me to flicker and then I heard a predictable crash from the lab where Vandermeer had knocked over a cage.

Nanobots formed a giant upright mouse of my own demented design, into which I downloaded and thundered to the lab. The copy of myself I'd left in the helm was continuing my anxiety attack as I worked to comfort the rats and put the cages back in order. Picking up the squirming cat, he immediately recognized me, no matter my bizarre appearance, and purred against my furry stomach.

"That's an alien civilization down there," I shakily told him. "A world as complex as our own. Well, this is what I'm here for, isn't it? Though I didn't quite expected it so soon."

The planet was buzzing with life. Mass communications and the sparkling diamond lights of cities. Though no space vehicles that I could detect. If they were advanced enough hundreds of years ago to visit the Dogon, what had happened? Could they detect me?

I set Vandermeer down, dissolved the giant mouse, and downloaded back into the helm.

Dimly and then not so dimly, I grew aware of a great consciousness flowing in and out of my own, a mind that made me feel the size of a peanut. I sensed immediately that this consciousness was incredibly evolved. A comparison might be the meeting of an archangel and an earthworm. Well, possibly this was showing a lack of self-esteem; more like an archangel and a squirrel.

The great alien psyche was watching and waiting.

Feebly I said, "Greetings. I have come only to observe and learn."

In response, it said to me (all over me, inside me, around me), "Jillian Stone. You have come out of curiosity to see your old

benefactor. We did indeed visit your world thousands of years ago and taught some of your people the rudiments of civilization. At that time, we came to help undo a great wrong done to your world by power hungry beings that, instead of allowing the natural unfolding of your species, injected their own DNA into your world's primitive hominids to rush their development. These beings then mined gold from your planet, using the new humans as slaves. Due to this genetic interference, your ancestors developed intellectually too quickly for their spiritual and ethical growth. The result is violent creatures who pollute their own world."

"What happened to those who interfered?" I managed to ask.

"The selfish ones left your world after stripping it of what they wanted. We came to do what we could to soften the damage. But I fear we did not do enough."

I felt sadness and love from this beautiful being. All I could think of to say was *thank you*.

"Now you can help us," it said.

"Help *you*?" I could feel nothing but my insignificance. "What could I possibly do for you?"

"On the planet you see below you, we were once the dominant corporeal species. Our form was something like a combination of your primate and amphibian. Over eons, we passed through the usual stages of civilization and levels of technology as your own species is doing. The difference is that renegade aliens had not tampered with us. We evolved at a natural pace.

"As species often do, we eventually joined with our technology, absorbed it and moved beyond until we no longer existed in physical reality. When we visited your world, we were on the brink. Eventually, our individual minds joined into the One. We now live and move in countless dimensions and join in Light with evolved civilizations from other fortunate worlds.

"We still have love for this, our planet, which exists in multidimensional states beneath our own, and all of the beings who inhabit these dimensions depend upon the continued wellbeing of each other. As is your own world, if only you were aware. Earth is not as simplistic as you believe."

"What do you mean?"

"You only see one level of reality. Many realms invisible to human eyes exist on Earth as well."

I was silent, trying to digest this.

"So, will you help us?"

What was I, a mere container in space, getting myself into? I knew that we owed them, but I was afraid. "All right," I finally said. "What can I do?"

A powerful rush of relief undulated through the Mind. "Once we left corporeal existence on our world, the scene was left open for another species to evolve to the top of the life chain. A certain animal we called Vasoda had acquired the use of primitive tools and was just discovering controlled fire. They had been leaving evidence of this in isolated places but we ourselves were undergoing such a wonderful metamorphosis that we did not pay attention.

"These beings, which do not resemble us as we were in physical form, have now reached the stage of technology which can bring destruction to our world. The cause of this particular destruction does not include, as on your planet, conflict and mass murder, but rather misjudgments in the use of technology."

"What are they doing?" I asked.

"The Vasoda are starting to employ sound or vibration to control the weather and protect crops from pests. They do not know that this use of vibration threatens the stability of the dimensional layers. In most inhabited worlds, a species either passes this stage of dangerous technologies or destroys itself, in which case it takes eons for the planet to recover. If the species passes, it moves to higher and higher levels of technology until it eventually transforms as we did and becomes invisible to those in lower levels. Each time a species steps up, more levels of reality are dependent upon the survival of the world. There comes a time when the evolution of trillions is at stake. Often the higher levels have to step in and place controls upon the lower."

"What do you want me to do?"

"For the most part, being in physicality inhibits receiving communications from higher levels of reality. There are individuals who possess the abilities to receive them, there are those who receive but refuse to listen, and there are those who listen but refuse to heed. On your world, do you not have those who claim to see angels? Does anyone heed their ranting in your modern times?"

I didn't need to respond.

"If individuals in *high positions* were to receive such communications, perhaps we can change the sweep of history. Perhaps we can ensure there will be more history to come."

I began to dimly understand what this being wanted.

"To the corporeal populace of this world, you would appear magical or divine. We ourselves can no longer manifest in their reality. But you still have the means to become the 'messenger from God.' Similar to what we once did for your own civilization."

Had I come from being an escapee from one civilization to being the savior of another? I felt a bit inadequate.

"Please explain to me how I am to accomplish this," I said and what followed was an hour of download straight into my consciousness.

Afterwards, I understood the layout of civilization on this world and several of their languages. There were six religions over twenty-three nations. All were having problems with agriculture and the weather was passing through a violent stage. The planet had oceans, as on earth, but the elements in the atmosphere were of a slightly different composition. Fortunately, I was using nano-bodies that could "breathe" anything.

I thought back to when Harper first explained this to me.

"Do not fear that you will be limited to the ship body," he'd said. "A nanobot fog will construct any form you desire for forays onto planets, space stations or other ships. You may scan the environment you wish to visit, program the nanos to construct a likely body for that milieu, create a copy of your personality and download it into the ship and download yourself into the nanobody."

We'd been speaking as if I already had the job. As if I had already accepted the fact that I would be giving up my life as a human.

But then I went and accepted the offer. And later, after the consciousness trans-ference had taken place, Harper smiled and said, "Now form a body, anything you like, and let's see how you do."

And so, I had downloaded myself into the exact copy of the currently reigning porn star, Veronica Raines, and strutted about in the cockiest manner I could manage. The body felt superb, strong, and invincible,

unlike anything I had ever experienced in my own of flesh and blood.

Now, light years from home, I formed an alien body using my instructions from the Mind. A mirror in the bridge afforded me a holographic view of it. It was fascinating to watch it take shape and I allowed myself a few moments to observe it before download-ing into it.

The figure was 2.13 meters tall with a head and four limbs in usual humanoid fash-ion. The shoulders were starkly slanted, the arms quite short, only reaching slightly below where a human waist would be if the creature actually had one. Instead there was a flat torso like a very thick board down to where it split into two legs. The legs them-selves were shapeless until they reached their lower end and bulged into muscle. They ended in two flat feet tipped with one big toe and a wide flat one. The creature's skin was gray-ish tan. Something resembling hair grew out of the head, perhaps more like furry scales. A small bump and two large holes for the nose, a wide gaping hole for the mouth, and lit-tle flaps over ear holes. The eyes were lovely. I had never seen such beautiful eyes. Large, wide, and tilted at the corners with glistening silver-white sclera and large, round irises of jade green flecked with gold. The eyes alone made me less reluctant to download into this otherwise quite ugly, at least to a human, character.

I did so forthwith, and the Mind said, "This is Galward, the avatar who came to Klewth fifteen hundred years ago and taught the ways of going inward to find oneself. While some followed his ways and lived humbly and in ecstasy, the majority of his followers set him up as a god and created endless meaningless rituals. But this is just part of the spiritual evolution of the species. As it now stands, a Galwardeen who is visited by a manifestation of his avatar will fall down in bliss or terror and be altered by the experience. You will now dress the figure in Galward's customary 'holy' garb."

Immediately, a robe fell over me and settled in quite fashionable folds. A belt of what appeared to be leather girded my nonexistent waist. Upon my hands, which ended in six digits and were spotted with brown blotches, appeared two rings: the one on my left of red-gold metal holding a black stone and on my right one of greenish white metal with a red stone.

"Galward wasn't into poverty, I take it?" I said.

"Not at all," replied my instructor.

I whirled around, checking my appearance in the fine clothing. "Am I considered attractive?"

"Galward is depicted by the masses as being more physically attractive than he actually was. I have given you the appearance the world has grown to believe he had. You are quite good-looking."

"Thank you," I said, finding that my face scrunched up under my huge eyes as I replied. "Is this the equivalent of a human smile?"

The Mind had evidently had enough of my shallow concerns and said, "You are to appear in the resting chamber of Preemis Wien, head environmental scientist for the Division of Eastern Loumis. I will give you the coordinates and you will appear there just as Preemis is drifting into his rest. You will startle him awake. Fortunately, he is alone as his two mates are visiting their families."

"What do I say to him?"

The Mind explained.

It amazed me how nanobodies were capable of all the emotional ups and downs of a living, natural body, though you could raise or lower the emotional or physical pain threshold if you desire. Pain is sometimes good to keep, as it can prevent you from knocking off appendages.

As Galward, I felt rather sweet and definitely kind.

I removed myself from this new and elegantly attired nanobody, reassembled it into an entry capsule, and fired it to the specific coordinates. Under the cover of night, the capsule dissolved into a nanobot fog that slipped under the door into the dwelling of Preemis Wien and then reassembled into the form of Galward. Immediately, my personality transmitted into the nanobody and I found myself inside Preemis' bedroom. I had appeared with a flourish by the side of what was probably his bed. These people slept curled over a large, soft hump on the floor, as a child might drape herself over a beach ball. But wait. Didn't the Mind tell me that the wives of this Preemis Wien were both away visiting relatives? Then who was the other being sharing his bed?

I tiptoed in the semi dark to take a closer look. One of the two beings was smaller and wore nothing while the other was my size and wearing a white tunic. Since both were lying on their "stomachs," I couldn't see if the smaller one had mammary glands or anything different from my own assumed male body. Was Preemis playing with a mouse while the cat was away?

A quick glance around gave me the layout and style of the room. The stone floor was covered here and there by brightly colored, woven mats, and the walls were hung with tapestries. Soft lighting ran along the floor and along the ceiling too, though this was presently turned off. Stubby, thick-leaved plants grew out of containers along one wall and a contraption containing lighted liquid bubbled in one corner. I could have sworn it was a twentieth century Earth lava lamp. I wanted to examine it, but the larger person suddenly stirred from his beach ball and rolled off onto the floor in a state of agitation. The other soon did the same and cowered, futilely trying to cover his/her nakedness.

"By the Fires of Tria, are you—?" the large one demanded, his great green eyes as beautiful as my own open wide in terror. He raised his hands in front of his face as if afraid I was going to strike him.

"You're Preemis?" I said.

"Yes," he squeaked.

Using as solemn and holy a voice I could muster, I replied, "I am your Lord, Galward, come to speak with my beloved follower."

The poor scientist prostrated himself upon the floor before me. I could see his back shaking with fear. He also stole a guilty glance at his cowering companion who was scuttling to disappear around the side of the bed.

"Rise up, Preemis, and regard me. I have come to give you a message from the Great Source!"

Preemis looked up but remained on his knees. I could tell that he'd hardly heard my words, he was so overcome with fright.

I gestured with one beringed hand, and Preemis begged, "May I kiss that hand, Beloved Master?"

I allowed him one kiss, a most pleasant experience. "Now Preemis," I said, "I have come to tell you that you must help me save the world. I need you to bring this great change about. And just to satisfy my curiosity, who is that other person there scrambling about?"

His coloring turned darker for a moment before he hesitatingly answered. "No one important, my Lord. Just a neighbor to keep me warm as I sleep."

"I see," I replied, suppressing a terrible urge to giggle. "But you know, Preemis, that everyone is important in the eyes of the Lord. I hope you haven't forgotten that."

He groveled. "Oh no, my Lord, I didn't mean . . . I am so sorry, I . . . but anything you ask, my Lord, I will do. Just ask!"

"Preemis, the technology that you and the others are using to protect the crops and direct the weather will ultimately cause great destruction to the world. I want you to stop it immediately."

He appeared confused. "You mean the use of ultra-low frequencies to clear the crops of pests? The low waves to arrest the storms?"

"That is indeed what I am referring to."

"You want me to *stop* it? To undo all the research, the planning, the—"

"I remind you that you said you would do anything I asked. I do not ask more of my followers than they can give."

He had the grace to look sorry. "Forgive me, Lord, I just need to know why. Could you please tell me why you are asking this?"

"If you allow this to continue, it will destroy the life on this world. I leave it to you to dismantle all your machines and find another method to achieve your ends, even if you must make sacrifices of a monetary and personal nature to do so. I am depending on you to save the world."

With that, I transmitted back to Quester. The nanobody was programmed to dissolve a microsecond later back into a fog and slip out any available crack in the wall or under a door where it would disperse and self-destruct. To Preemis, it would appear that I had vanished.

"Well done," said the Mind. "Although we wonder if the hand kissing was necessary. Do forgive me for not checking for neighborly visits. And now for your next assignment . . ."

This one took me to a large wooden sea vessel in a very pleasant tropical location. Moored near a reef, its sailors were enjoying a swim in a nearby lagoon while overhead draped the long branches of what looked like palm trees, a scene reminiscent of earth's South Pacific. The giant suns were setting and soon, I figured, the sailors would drink their grog or whatever these people did and drunkenly nod off to sleep. That would free me up to confront the captain's guest, Machne, the Supreme Commander of Lobreen, a large country directly east of this idyllic scene.

I was about to find out that the Mind, though far-reaching, was not omnipotent. The captain apparently had no intention of allowing his guest to do such a mundane thing as go to his "bunk" and sleep.

"Come on, Machne, remember our days at school, how we played Ten Questions all night long and each question got us more intoxicated than the last?"

He passed his guest a glass sphere of green, undulating gas with a short tube projecting from it and Machne quietly accepted it with both hands. While I thought I saw a gleam of desperation in the Supreme Commander's eyes, he obligingly bent his head and inhaled through the little tube.

"Now, question number one," said the Captain.

I, appearing as Windred, the fierce female leader of the ancient Lobreenians who taught her followers that sacrificing oneself in battle assured one of a direct flight to paradise, was lurking in my leather battle getup in a very cramped closet between the Captain's quarters and what would be Machne's, if he were permitted to go to bed.

"Good idea of yours to take a break from politics," boomed the Captain. "Maybe it's time for you to hand over the reins to your son."

"Hmmmmm," mumbled Machne, and just as I peeked through a large crack in the wall, the closet door was ripped open and I was face to face with the Captain.

"I thought I heard something in there," he bellowed while drawing a spikey looking weapon. Then he put his fingers in his mouth and made a god-awful whistle that brought the thumping of sailors' feet to his door.

He couldn't really hurt me—I could move my nanobots to allow a sharp point to enter my body without harm—but getting caught in this way was not conducive to accomplishing the mission. Apparently, the Mind had assumed Machne would be asleep by now and alone.

"Who is this intruder?" yelled the Captain into my face as he grabbed my arm. Did he not recognize me from the many religious pictures all over his nation and on the wall of his own quarters?

Two brutal looking sailors burst into the quarters and soon were locking me into double iron handcuffs. "Shall we throw her overboard?" asked the one on my right.

Machne, in the haze of whatever he had inhaled, turned to look at me and then gasped. "My Lady, oh my Lady!" He got up, stumbled and fell to his knees. "Let her go, you fools! Do you not see who she is?"

The Captain stood back and looked at me. "My Lady, forgive me," he said as he too dropped to his knees. The sailors followed suit.

Over the next rotation of the planet, I made four more visitations to selected persons on different landmasses. I was Blanneck, who taught self-sacrifice as the road to ecstasy; Trahorn who instructed her followers in the pleasures of giving; Valeen who once promoted the cleansing of the spirit through sexual union and offspring rearing, and Sibo who healed people by staring into their eyes. In a blaze of light, I entered their chambers, struck fear and awe into their souls, and ordered the salvation of their world in whatever capacity they had to bring that about. I did run into another neighborly visit, outraged pets, and a chamber without an escape route where I had to hide in a latrine, but I got the jobs done.

"I think I need to shut down and coast a bit," I told the Mind. "I need quiet and my cat. It was extremely good fun though. Did it work, do you think?"

In answer, I received a giant caress as if my entire psyche was enveloped in warm, pulsating light.

"It should hold them at bay for a while," said the Mind. "Hopefully, they can come up with better solutions to the environmental problems."

"And if they don't?" I asked.

"Perhaps someone at your present level of development will pass by and we can pull them in to help us as we did you."

"You pulled me in?"

"We influenced. You could have chosen anywhere. We can only influence."

"I want to know something," I said. "Earth is like your planet? All the layers, the moving up of species? Is that what you meant about it being more complex than we imagine?"

"It is."

I was bursting with questions. "What species will move up to take our place? Is it the chimps? The crows? The dolphins? How many species have evolved above us? How long will it take us to change?"

"One has moved beyond you. And nothing is assured. Your species is faulty as I mentioned before—the selfishness, the violence. Nothing is certain, but one can hope."

It took me days to recover. There was so much to digest.

This time was, for me, a private celebration. For now I understood that we humans had not reached the end of the line, that there was potential and adventure left to us after all.

I floated in the sparkling black and in my way, smiled.

Margaret Karmazin's credits include stories published in literary and sci-fi magazines, including Rosebud, Chrysalis Reader, North Atlantic Review, Mobius, Confrontation, Pennsylvania Review, The Speculative Edge and Another Realm. Her stories in The MacGuffin, Eureka Literary Magazine, Licking River Review and Mobius were nominated for Pushcart awards. She has stories included in several anthologies, published a YA novel, Replacing Fiona, a children's book, Flick-Flick & Dreamer, and a collection of short stories, Risk.

THE RENTED ROOM

VIRGINIA BETTS

IT IS COMMONLY understood that along with a birth, a death, and a divorce, moving house is one of life's most stressful events. I had no close, personal experience of the first three, but I was ready to risk the last, as the time had come to move on. Feeling the familiar impulse to start looking over my shoulder once again, I sold my place of solitary refuge and was about to take flight to the other end of the country. A writer, always hoping to add one more chapter to my own tale, it was entirely fitting that I was here, almost ready to leave, boxing up my treasured books.

As I picked up the last dust-covered book and placed it carefully into the box, I found myself considering again that night so long ago. I sat surrounded by cardboard vessels filled with printed tales to delight and horrify, but of all the stories I have written and read, none made such an indelible mark on my life as the story I became a part of some forty years ago. It seemed like only days back that the terrible events unfolded around me, although a lifetime had withered and died in those same hours and minutes.

No, I was not the same person who had embarked on my journey all those years previously. The mirror that once reflected a face full of hope and promise now framed a weary, aging visage with eyes clouded by fear and defeat. I checked the book I had just placed into the box, almost as if it would reveal a secret to me or point me to a destiny I had yet to reach. It was a collection of poetry by Philip Larkin. I knew the poems it contained. One of them, "Mr. Bleaney," beginning "This was Mr. Bleaney's room," reminded me of the landlady's words to me when I'd had arrived in Paradise Street on that fateful day.

It had been an uneventful journey to reach my destination that day. I had taken the train in the morning and then found myself, by means of a newly purchased map, rounding the corner into Paradise Street, the location housing the address I sought. The street was ordinary enough; perhaps it was a little narrow, but otherwise, a quiet and orderly area. I strode with a spring in my step. Newly qualified as a schoolteacher, and having commenced writing my first novel with an advance from a publisher, I felt that life offered me a wealth of treasures to uncover, and even the wintry wind at my collar did not unduly irk me. The map flapped in the wind as I tried to check my location was correct and, as I did so, I skidded on a patch of hidden ice.

"Bugger!" I exclaimed, hurriedly looking around to check that no one had spotted my ignominious slide. I regained my composure, glad I had not fallen to the wet ground, and stopped walking. I looked up and down the long street. I smiled at the irony of the street name: 'Paradise' it was not! It was simply an ordinary street, containing the usual rows of houses and shops, some cheerful and some dreary, all hunched up together as if comforting each other against the cold. One building, however, stood out from the rest. It looked as if it belonged to another time and seemed to assert its own individual character on the street. It was

a shop front with a classical-style protruding glass window, divided into small panes. The mullions, sill, cornices, and fascia were all painted in maroon, and the display inside showcased rows and rows of books, of eclectic style and genre, almost beckoning the customer inside. Despite the wintry sun, the interior looked old and dark, yet the books gave the shop color and vibrancy, and I was intrigued. I checked the map for my location as I knew the address I sought was in this street. I checked the address again. It seemed that the address of the flat I planned to view that day was right here in this bookshop!

There was no one in sight to ask, and, as the weather was so cold, I decided that my best chance was to go inside the bookshop and see if there was anyone who could shed some light on the situation. I peered at the sign above the door. In large, gold-leaf letters, it read: 'Eden Books.' Underneath, in smaller lettering, it read, 'Proprietor, Mr. Carstairs Nile, Esq.' I tried the door and it swung open easily, caught by the wind, and precipitating the jingle of the bell above the door to alert the assistant to customers.

"Excuse me," I said, timidly. "Is there anyone around who can help me? I'm supposed to look at a flat here, but the address seems to match this bookshop."

At that moment, a flustered-looking woman, middle-aged and shabbily dressed came hurrying into the shop. "Are you Mr. Fairfax?" she inquired, "Because you have got the right place, it's just that there is a side door leading into the flats and it's hidden from the street if you don't know the area. I must have forgotten to mention it, but it's difficult to explain really, if you don't know it. Do come through. I'm Janet

Underworth, the landlady, technically. I live in the flat at the back and the one you're after is upstairs. Come through, I've got the keys and full approval to show you round."

I paused. "Who is Mr. Nile then? Does he own the bookshop?"

"To be honest, not many people ever get to meet Mr. Carstairs in person. Oh, sorry, I mean Mr. Nile. I always call him Mr. Carstairs, on account of mistaking his Christian name for his Surname when I first met him. It sort of stuck. Sounds good as well! So, he owns the bookshop, yes, and also the flats really, but because he is always travelling so much, picking up new stock and so forth, I keep the place for him and act as Landlady. I work in the shop, look after the tenant upstairs and make sure all his affairs here are in order. He's not a marrying type, so, as you can imagine, the place needs a woman to keep things ticking over. Come on then!" She beckoned for me to cross the threshold properly and go after her.

I followed her through the bookshop, weaving my way between the dusty shelves and dangling oriental lampshades. I was an avid reader, naturally, given my dual professions, and I had literally hundreds of books of all types and subjects. But this bookshop seemed stocked to the brim with tomes I would be happy to spend hours poring over. There was hardly room to pass between the shelving and, as I negotiated them, somehow one or two of them fell despite my care, and I stooped to replace them. The dusty and leathery aroma filled my nostrils and I reflected that, like the name of the street, this to me was paradise, of a sort.

Ever since I was a child, it was almost a forgone conclusion that I would be destined to become either a writer or a keeper of books.

I had been obsessed with them, devouring their contents as soon as I could read, being transported to other worlds and far off lands in my head. I qualified as a teacher to ensure that I had a sensible career with which to provide myself and a future family an income, but I had chosen English because I felt I could also imbue other young minds with the same love of literature. I found my first job in this small and insignificant town and had come to find a place to live before the start of term, as the Summer shifted into Autumn, and the days brought with them an unexpected, premature, wintry cold snap.

"This was Mr. Hogarth's Room," said the landlady. "He stayed here the whole time he worked in the town, until they took him away."

"Was that a long time then?" I inquired.

"Ooh, he came here when the flat was done up new—it wasn't a flat before; I think it was used for storing all the books. Anyway, when I took over as landlady here and had my same flat downstairs at the back, it wasn't in any fit state to let really. But Mr. Hogarth, he was happy to take it and do it up a bit."

I glanced around the flat. I felt as if the room's own mood was overwhelming me. A dour, melancholy spirit, a pulsating, lacklustre sigh seemed to heave from every corner. I breathed in the damp, musty aroma. I noted the faded, frayed curtains, and the lack of care apparent in the rest of the upholstery—a torn sofa, faded nets, moth-eaten bedding piled up. It was, in its own way, a relic, exuding a testament to an age of monochrome. The landlady, like the accommodation she had to offer, reeked of the past and seemed to carry with her the room's same taint of neglect. Small clues left around the flat—many such cheap trophies from the same seaside town, a couple of photographs, a few scattered newspaper articles in drawers—revealed that he was not a man who had ever ventured far. However, she seemed entranced by her erstwhile tenant.

"Oh, he stayed here for such a long time," she chattered on, "even," and here she leaned towards me conspiratorially, "even *after* he passed. It was more than a week he lay." She spoke in a whisper, reverentially.

I looked again at the frayed curtains, the holes, the stairs. Even the furniture was decades behind its time, cheap and never chic. Behind the door was a single coat hook. The landlady continued to chatter, her words fading in and out of my consciousness as I surveyed the box-like surroundings.

"Oh, he was such a lovely, helpful man. He took such great care of this place you know. He did wonders for my little patch of land. Course, it really all belongs to Mr. Carstairs, but he never comes and it's as good as mine."

She drew back the decrepit netting, even as I marvelled at her obliviousness. Daylight broke into the murky gloom in watery shards of sunlight, infiltrating areas that appeared not to have seen the light of day, possibly for decades. Insects retreated like vampires to their coffins, woodlice and stray spiders scurried to the corners and under the floorboards as the day invaded.

I peered at the aforementioned patch of land out the window. The sight that greeted me was not altogether unexpected, given the nature of the room and its caretaker. The 'patio,' if it could be called that, was a concrete crazy paving riddled with weeds slyly springing up between the cracks. The 'land' backing onto this overgrown area had long

since defied any description connected with the word 'lawn.' Reeds of grass shot skyward as high as a seven-year-old, riddled with yellowing weeds and straw and unknown plants. A rusty watering can sat dryly in one corner and a brown-handled rake in another. I looked from room to land and back again, and the two scenes became almost interchangeable in my mind. Despite this, I turned to the landlady and spoke.

"Well," I said, "your previous guest *did* stay here a long time, he obviously felt at home, so . . . I'll take it."

I was soon settled in, having moved as many of my things as I could up in suitcases hauled on and off the train and trundled through the streets. The rest I arranged to be delivered by road transport. Now, a fortnight later, I was still unpacking, but the neglected room that wore such a melancholy air began to come to life. It still bore the terrible décor and murky appearance that it inherited from its predecessor, but I stamped some of my own personal taste on the room and, crucially, I now had my books about me.

I started term, met my classes with the well-prepared eagerness of a new member of staff and found it to be rewarding, if exhausting, work. I was sometimes disappointed that others did not think in the same way, and that my young charges in the days of my training seemed more interested in trivia, sport, and dating than the works of Dickens and Shakespeare. But there were one or two who had been genuinely interested and had shown promise. I felt I could make a difference. I even had time to continue with my own writing a little, in the happy state that I had plenty of time to fulfil my requirements for that contract as they had already liked the first ten thousand words of the manuscript I had sent.

That Friday evening, I took up my position on the sofa with a glass of whiskey and a book to read, unusually, purely for my own leisure. The weekend beckoned, and I joyfully remembered that I had made plans to visit the cinema the next night, along with a very pretty and earnest young colleague named Mary Martin. In my mind, I was making the most of what life had to offer me so far.

As I read, I grew steadily sleepier by the glowing firelight. I was beginning to find it difficult to distinguish between what I was reading on the page, and what I knew to be reality, and I must have dozed off, with vivid images of Poe's ghostly tale haunting my dreams. I woke to find the flat in darkness and I could hear a strange, intermittent thudding sound coming from downstairs. I wondered what on earth Miss Underworth could be doing, but then I remembered that she was away for the weekend. I jumped up and tried to switch the lamp on, but it seemed that the lightbulb had blown, and I remained disorientated and in blackness. I felt around for my lighter on the old coffee table and knocked an old ashtray, which had evidently belonged to Mr. Hogarth, onto the floor. Eventually grasping hold of my lighter, I flicked it with shaking hands. The flame flickered, sputtered, and died. I tried again and this time the eerie orange glow illuminated the area with a tiny light. Shapes wavered and distorted, and as I tried to move across the room, I almost dropped the lighter with a start. What I thought was a phantom was only a glimpse of myself in the looking glass above the fireplace.

Eventually, I made it to the main light switch, but when I flicked it, even that did not yield any light. I began to feel the first prickles of panic creeping across my skin. I

stood still in the darkness, aware of my own breathing becoming faster and shallower, and I had difficulty controlling my racing thoughts while I considered what to do. My eyes were growing accustomed to the blackness, so, with the aid of my ailing lighter flame, I slowly began to side-step toward the door to make my way to the top of the stairs in the hall.

The long, narrow corridor beckoned, and I groped my way along it, using the wall as support and guidance. All the time I edged closer to the stairs, the dull thudding sound continued, growing more insistent with every tentative step I took. It seemed to mimic the sound of the footsteps of a slow and heavy beast, first a slide, and then a thud, repeating itself again and again, over and over, never changing pace, but growing louder and more menacing as I moved towards it.

Finally, I reached the staircase, felt the bulbous wooden post of the bannister and, despite the failing flame and the looming shadows cast along the wall and ceiling, I stepped gingerly out. One step . . . two steps . . . holding on tightly, all the time the rhythmic thudding growing ever more insistent. At the last step, I missed my footing and dropped my lighter into the blackness with an echoing metallic clang. I breathed in. Time seemed suspended. I dared not move; the thud had stopped.

Breathing heavily and with pounding heart, I sprinted to where I approximated the hall light to be and flicked it. It was a dim lantern, but after the pitch blackness, it seemed to flood the hallway with brilliance. The light showed nothing out of place, and I stood for a moment to gather my wits, then made my way through into the bookshop itself, flicking on the dull lanterns as I went, fearing an encounter with I knew not what.

My imagination was in riotous overdrive, yet I tried to rationalize my thoughts.

Finally, I came to the last of the shelves in the claustrophobic little area—before me lay an enormous pile of books, scattered about my feet on the floor, as if they had been pushed from the shelves one by one by the fingers of an invisible force. Now the hackles on my neck began to rise, and a slow chill began to spread up my spine, like tiny, icy footsteps along my back.

For a moment I felt frozen to the spot, but for some unfathomable reason, my first reaction was to bend and pick the books up to place them back on the shelves. As I did so, another fell, or, and I had little doubt of this, was pushed, and struck me a blow in the neck. I straightened up and turned sharply; one after another of the books began to fly from their housing, lobbed at my face and head with some force. I no longer wanted to stay and tidy up! I dashed for the back of the shop and rushed up the stairs again, tripping and stumbling over my own feet in my panic, and did not pause until I had re-entered my dark flat and slammed the door. Catching my breath, I fumbled for the light switch, forgetting that it had not worked before. I snapped it on and, oddly, this time it lit up the room.

Glad to be back in the light, I relaxed a little, although I was still shaken. But my respite was short-lived. As my eyes met with the mirror above the fireplace, it appeared to be steamed up, and in the centre, one word stood out: *LEAVE*.

In the few days that followed, I kept the incident to myself, trying to rationalize what had happened. But I cannot pretend that I wasn't unsettled. The next morning, I returned to the scene of the night's disturbance, thinking about how I might explain the scattered books to Mrs. Underworth when she returned. However, the books had been placed back on the shelves. This was even more unnerving, and I searched for footprints, signs of a break-in, or even the remnants of some ghostly ectoplasm dripping from the shelves. But there were no signs, and I began to wonder if I had imagined it all.

No more disturbances occurred for a while, and I continued with life, working and developing a nice little relationship with Mary Martin. It was fun at school, snatching odd moments between classes, dodging the curious eyes of the children, making dates to see films and have dinner: 'courting,' as they still called it in those days.

One evening, standing at my shaving mirror and preparing to meet Mary in the town, I suddenly felt an icy chill creep up my back. It was not unusual to feel cold, as Winter had seemed to have the country in its icy grip since September with no plans to depart, but this was not the weather. The shiver making my skin crawl was familiar.

I laid down my cut-throat razor but kept it close. I felt the room grow cold, and my breath condensed on exhalation. It fell so silent that I could hear my own blood pumping round my body, and I was aware of every organ working overtime. I began to hear creaking on the stairs, like footsteps of someone approaching slowly whilst trying to remain hushed.

I dared not leave the bathroom, but I listened as the steps seemed to move across the floor of my flat, even as the room I was in appeared to become enveloped in shadow. The bathroom began to steam up. I moved to pick up the razor blade again, but it was not where I had placed it. Suddenly, I felt a sharp, stinging sensation, and watched in horror as two words appeared to be carved into the flesh of my torso: *GET OUT!* The world began to spin around me, and everything went black.

When I awoke, Mary and Mrs. Underworth were standing over me with a cup of tea.

"Don't talk," said Mary. "It's all right."

"Just like poor Mr. Hogarth," said Mrs. Underworth.

"Ssh!" said Mary and turned to me. "Doctor is on his way."

Later, I found myself in a hospital bed, trying to piece together what had happened.

"So, you can't remember anything?" asked the Doctor.

"Not really, but I didn't do this," I cringed, indicating my bandaged chest. "I know it sounds ridiculous, but it seemed to happen by itself, like someone was doing it to me."

The man in the white coat raised his eyebrows. "Someone will be along to speak to you tomorrow," he said, "when you feel better."

"Overworked," was the verdict. "Stressed and too much to do with the new school and the book." Discussions about my 'fragile mental health,' and 'repressed grief from childhood leading to depressive tendencies,' had taken place, and I was cautiously released with medication. Mary promised to keep an eye on me, but I noticed that her affections had cooled a little.

"Mary," I said, when she was visiting one evening, "do you believe in ghosts?" I saw her face written all over with skepticism and surprise, but I proceeded to explain my experiences. "Also," I went on, "other things have happened, now I think about it. Things I can't explain. Just little things, like things going missing and turning up in the wrong place. And my constant lack of energy. What do you think Mrs. Underworth meant by, 'just like Mr. Hogarth?'"

"I don't know, Jacob, but all of those things sound like the stress the Doctors talked about. I hope you're not going mad!"

"Mary, will you stay with me tonight?" I asked tentatively. "Not like that, I'll sleep in here, but I just don't feel entirely safe anymore, and it always seems to happen when Mrs. Underworth is away."

"All right," she replied.

It must have been the noise that woke me around two in the morning. This time, I was able to snap the lamp on. I could hear it again—thud . . . thud . . . thud. I started to rise to wake Mary, but she was already by my side.

"What is that, Jacob?" she whispered in alarm.

"That's the noise I heard before! If we go down with a torch, I bet we will find the books being thrown about again!"

We crept down the passage and descended the stairs. My hand shook as I held the heavy torch, lighting our way into the shop. Sure enough, the books were scattered about. Mary gasped when she saw them. Slowly I shone the torch along the empty shelves.

Suddenly, I jumped back in fear as a grim face loomed up opposite me. It was a pale, narrow face, with sharp cheekbones, aquiline features, and a high forehead. I cried out in terror!

"Good evening, Sir, Madam. I am so sorry to startle you. I just arrived from overseas. My name is Carstairs Nile."

After that first meeting, Mr. Nile stayed for a few weeks. He was charming when he

conversed with us, although his tall, imposing figure always made me feel uneasy,
intimidated perhaps, by his not inconsider-
able intellect. He seemed to glide between
the bookshelves, sometimes speaking to the
customers, who were rare indeed, more often
reading or cataloguing his wares. Mostly, I
avoided him—he seemed to keep odd hours,
seldom did he move outside the shop during
daylight, and as I was working again and
typing up my manuscript at the weekend,
I rarely crossed paths with him or Janet
Underworth.

Which was why I was so surprised to see
him at my door one winter evening. "Good
evening," he said. "I thought I would come
introduce myself formally. I am sorry I startled you when I arrived. How are you settling in
here? Is Mrs. Underworth taking care of you?"

"To be honest, I don't see her very often.
I have been so busy, you see, with my work
and my book—which I regret to say I am
behind with. But do come in."

"Ah. Your predecessor was also a writer.
Full of energy. He loved being above the
bookshop—he was drawn to it like a moth
to a flame."

"Was he really? Do tell me more—Mrs.
Underworth seemed to adore him, but from
what I can see, from the little trinkets he left
around the place, he seems to have been a bit
of an old stick-in-the-mud!"

"Ah yes. Well, he never did finish anything properly as time went on. Got
somewhat depressed shall we say? Lost all
his enthusiasm."

"A shame, maybe?" I replied, warily.
"Anyway, would you like a drink, Sir?"

"Carstairs, please. No, I won't keep you
from your business. But if you need anything,
Janet is under strict instructions!"

"Thank you, Mr. Niles." Somehow, the
first-name terms seemed far too informal for
such an imposing character. "There is one
thing though. Did Hogarth, or anyone else
for that matter, ever report any disturbances
around the place? In the bookshop?"

"Disturbances? No. But Mr. Hogarth himself was very disturbed. Killed himself in the
end, I'm sorry to say."

"I didn't know that. I am sorry to hear it.
Well thank you for visiting me. Next time do
stay for a drink."

"Good evening to you," he said once again.

I was taken with his formal tone. As with
much of the building itself, he seemed to
belong to a past age, yet he did not suffer the
sense of neglect that I had encountered when
I first arrived there. However, about Mr.
Hogarth I was intrigued. Maybe there was
something of his restless spirit still stalking
the flat.

The following day, I went to the library. I
did not really know what I expected to find,
but I scoured relentlessly through all the old
newspaper reports on record. Eventually, I
came to a small headline detailing the sui-
cide of Mr. James Hogarth, a horror writer
of small fame locally, who had been found
dead in his apartment above Eden Books in
Paradise Street. He had cut his wrists with a
razor blade. Once a promising writer, he had
gradually declined into mental breakdown,
believing that characters from his own stories had come to life and were out to kill him.
According to the reports, it seemed that he
had given up writing and become reclusive,
too afraid to leave the flat, and declining into
a form of schizophrenia until his death.

It was certainly intriguing, but what
really leapt out at me was the manner of his
death. A razor blade! My thoughts began to

stir in my brain and, despite trying to suppress such irrational fantasy, I could not help but wonder.

"So, you think Mr. Hogarth is haunting this flat and picking on you because he's jealous of your writing? Oh, come on!" scoffed Mary. "Now I *do* think you're crazy!"

"Mary, think about it! I can't explain what happened, and I am feeling so tired, I feel like I'm diminishing slowly. I can't work properly, I've been off work for ages, I've only just gone back to school, and I can't concentrate. It's like he's possessing me or something!"

"But there's been no more 'hauntings'? No more bumps in the night? Surely your landlady or that owner person—Nile isn't it? Surely they would have noticed it by now? I think we *can* explain it—you got tired, stressed and ill. You were depressed, moving house and all, the stress got to you—you had a breakdown."

"But, Mary, there was no reason for it—not really."

"Your mother died when you were young, and you never got over it properly. That's what they all talked about with you. You're getting better—we just have to keep an eye on you."

"I got over it! I grieved when I was a child!" I protested. "But it's not something within me, it's something outside of me."

But Mary remained unconvinced and not that sympathetic. She left earlier than usual that evening and I felt forlorn. I poured myself a whiskey and stared into the fire.

The whiskey began to be a regular addition to my evenings. Instead of working on my book, or preparing schoolwork, I would pour a drink, and then another. Just enough to send me into a stupor that enabled me to

sleep. But I did not sleep soundly. Every night after Mr. Nile left again, the noises would begin. The thudding, and now whispering, and a feeling of fingers lightly brushing my cheek. I could not distinguish between work and sleep. I heard voices, and the foggy nights seemed to infiltrate my room. Mary had abandoned me—I was a drunk with no ambition in her view. I was failing at my school job and on probation, and I missed the first deadline for my book. I could hardly find the energy to raise my head from my pillow these days. By February, I felt as if I had lost the will to live.

It was in the early hours of a Sunday night that I heard the noises again downstairs and I felt I'd had enough. With a final surge of the energy I had left, I hauled myself out of bed and across the room. I made my way downstairs as quietly as I could, determined, in my almost insane state, to find out what it was once and for all.

It all happened so fast, and yet it felt like a warped, slow-motion film. I took a step forward into the back of the shop, and with one swift movement, an horrific, cadaverous face was thrust into mine.

"Get out! Now!" the monster hissed. I realized, with horror, that this withered, consumptive vision was the face of Mr. Hogarth.

I screamed and ran forward. But what confronted me next was far worse. I saw the dark figure of Mr. Carstairs Nile hovering above the ground over the prostrate body of an unknown victim, with Mrs. Underworth looking on salaciously. Nile appeared to be draining the body, not of blood, but in an equally vampiric manner, of energy and life. The body shrank and became empty, almost as if its innards were melting away, leaving only the shell. The predators turned and fixed me with malevolent, red-eyed stares. I had no doubt, now, that I would be next.

They began to move towards me, and in my sickness and horror, I felt my legs almost buckle.

"Jacob," breathed Nile, "do not fear it. If you stay, you need not die. I just need your energy to survive, as I have done for all this time. It was clever of Mrs. Underwood to find you—she has served me all these years, so faithfully, and in return, she lives. I fed on Hogarth and he was able to live, but in the end, I needed someone younger, more vibrant. You can help me, Jacob, you can help me to live again."

He reached out, and his iron grasp clamped upon my arm. I almost accepted defeat, but then, from behind us, the books began to fly from the shelves and, in the confusion, a strong shove in the back propelled me forward and towards the front door. I grappled with the handle, fumbling at the lock, and, as I did so, I saw behind me, reflected in the windowpane, the pale face of Mr. Hogarth. "Go!" he mouthed. And I ran.

And so, as I packed my boxes today, once more on the move, I remembered Hogarth, and Eden books, and Paradise Street.

Again, the same feeling of dread swept over me. I glanced again at the poetry anthology, and as I did so, a book on the very top of the box caught my eye. It was Hogarth's own book, the only one he had finished, a copy I had secured from a charity shop. It was titled, 'Dark entity,' and was the story of an unknown creature that stalked the centuries, surviving on the life-energy of others. I shuddered, yet I reflected that, unlike Hogarth, I did finish my books, had seen them published. I remembered Mary, though, whom I had never seen again after that night. I do not know what became of Carstairs Nile, or Janet Underworth. For all I know, they might still be at Eden books, draining the energy out of more hapless victims, just enough to let them live, and in the process, crushing their hopes, dreams and ambitions. I do not know if James Hogarth will ever rest in peace.

I took one last glance at my lined and drawn face in the mirror, then I removed it from the wall and put it into a separate box. Outside, the van had arrived to take my belongings to my new destination. And so, alone, I went along the hallway, and opened the front door.

Virginia graduated from Essex University with a degree in Literature, and later gained a postgraduate degree in teaching English. She taught for 15 years, then set up her tuition business, Results Tutoring, where she indulges her passion for literary analysis whilst helping her students to achieve their potential. Alongside this, she has begun to have poetry, articles and short stories published. She has a passion for the Gothic genre, and loves all things Victorian. Her other obsessions are swimming and violin playing. Virginia discovered she had Asperger's syndrome late in life, which may contribute to the vivid worlds in her head—she often dreams stories or poems, getting up to write them at very unsociable hours! Virginia is married, with one son, aged 18.

Making Faces At A Baby On The Bus

ANDREY PISSANTCHEV

YOU'VE PROBABLY WALKED past me on the street many times. I go out for a stroll every day, and never get bored. I've been around for a while—and I've learned to get enjoyment out of the simplest things.

It is springtime, cool and sunny, parks lined with trees in bloom. I go past elderly couples walking hand in hand and office workers rushing back in after a quick cigarette break, salesmen hawking phone cases and cheap sunglasses.

All of them are complete strangers and yet, they all seem familiar. I pick out traits that I've seen before, a regal slope of the nose or a sensual thickness of the lips. Maybe it belongs to the niece or great-grandson of someone I've seen long ago. Or it could just be one of those coincidences, like an archetype that manifests itself regardless of race or nationality.

I spend a lot of time looking at faces. It's part of what I do. I take note of those subtle patterns, memorize them, sketch them out when I return home. I take pride in my attention to detail, and that's what makes my work so believable. You've probably walked past me on the street many times, and not suspected a thing.

Of course, I don't take it all too seriously. There's a lot of fun to be had. It comes with the territory.

I'm on a bus now. The commuter rush is over, and the late morning sun reflects off the empty seats. There's a mother in the seat in front of me, facing the direction of travel. She's tapping away at her phone, and her baby is looking back over her shoulder, visibly bored. I glance around. All other passengers are glued to their devices. An opportunity presents itself.

I tilt my head to catch its attention. When it notices me, I grin, raising my eyebrows comically. The baby is old enough to understand my expression, and it beams a smile back at me.

Without moving my eyebrows, I pull the corners of my mouth down in a grimace, exposing my bottom teeth. The baby gurgles with delight. It's enjoying the show so far.

I follow up with a lopsided pout and a cross-eyed stare, after which I flare my nostrils and move my ears all at the same time. My audience of one is enthralled.

At this point I pause, as any great entertainer will do before stepping up their act. I cover my face with my hands and when I remove them, I have taken the look of the bus driver, a jolly overweight man with a bright ginger beard. The baby squeals, pleased by the colors, and waves its hands in a way which I choose to interpret as applause.

I place my left palm above my face and sweep down, returning to my previous look, but I also add a twist: as I uncover my mouth, I reveal an outrageous black moustache. It sticks out to the sides and swoops down, rigid like the jaws of a beetle. I indulge in the similarity, opening and closing its halves soundlessly.

I squeeze my eyes shut, and they disappear completely. They open on my cheeks instead. I retract my facial hair, while my eyes start shifting about, chasing each other around my nose.

Throughout this performance, the baby watches me with glee. I'm a bit disappointed. I would have expected it to be in tears by now. So, I decide to take things a bit further. I know just the thing—it nearly drove a priest insane back in 1635.

I relax and bring my face back to normal. Then I focus. I let three thorns grow out, two at my cheek bones and one on my forehead. At the same time, my teeth grow sharper and my face elongates, turning a green tinge. The protrusions on my face stretch out into spikes, curving towards the baby's skull.

I pause. Nothing! The baby mumbles to itself, still smiling. I return to my old face plus a furrowing of the eyebrows I do not quite intend.

I plan out my next steps, but then I notice the baby is looking at me. Not the normal unfocused baby gaze. It looks at me dead on, with a hint of slyness in its face, like it wants to show me something.

I narrow my eyes. *Go on.*

The baby blinks, and when its eyes open, they are jet black. I sit up straight. It's an old trick, but not one I expected. Not from what appears to be a baby on the bus, at least. My curiosity is piqued. Even better, I sense a game of one-upmanship is afoot. So I wink with my left eye, then right, turning the first one deep blue, the second brilliant red. I then open scores of tiny eyes all over my face in a dazzling display of colors.

Your move, kid.

The baby tilts its head and chuckles in a way that seems completely unbabylike. As I watch, I find its eyes seem larger, even though they haven't increased physically in size. I lean in to get a closer look. Within the blackness I notice clusters of white dots. No, not dots. Stars. I make out more and more of them, cold points in a vast and uncaring starscape. I am no longer observing, I am within, moving at a great speed.

Before I can get my bearings, I am flung into a nearby planet. Clouds roll past me, thick and impenetrable. I push through. I fly above dead streets now. Flashes of lightning illuminate the concrete ruins beneath me. I realize the pale shapes on the ground are human bones, hundreds of them.

Familiarity dawns as I notice the shape of the city, the blighted parks, the remnants of office buildings. *I know this place.* I look ahead in anticipation. I can tell where I'm headed already. My own apartment block, still miraculously standing. I fly closer to a window, and recognize the figure moving within. It's me.

I wear the same face I'm wearing right now, but my clothes and belongings are in tatters. I study my own expression, observe my body language. My shoulders are hunched up, and my arms tremble as they move. My eyes are empty. There are no physical wounds on my body, but I know I am broken.

My other self is holding something. A long rope. There is a look of resolve on my face as I turn it into a noose. I see myself attach it to the ceiling, then slip it around my neck.

The world lurches around me, and I scream. I find myself back on the bus. I am on the floor and everybody is looking at me. I don't know whether the baby is still facing me. I can't bear to look. My head is splitting. I can taste blood in my mouth.

I feel the bus slowing down. I don't know if it reached a stop or a red light. I bang on the door until it opens, then scramble out.

I somehow make my way back to my flat. I look at the mirror, and the reflection that looks back is a distorted, melted thing. I pull myself together and mold my face into something more proper. I sigh. I think I'll need to go into hiding for a decade or two.

One thing is certain. I'm not going to play games with strangers ever again.

Andrey is a Bulgarian living in Leeds, UK. By day he works as a programmer. By other times of the day, he writes. By night, he waits. His short stories have appeared in Factor Four Magazine, Mystery Tribune and Grotesque Magazine, among others. You can find more of his work at https://write.as/andrey-p.

ROB BUTLER

Litter

AS I WAS growing up, Grandpa would never talk about The Pulse, no matter how many times I asked him about it. This really bugged me, as he was one of the few people still around who must have actually seen it. None of the other old farmers we knew would speak about it either. Not that we saw them very often. Too far to walk.

All I got were vague hints here and there.

We'd be fishing in the creek and after a long spell of silence, Grandpa would suddenly say something like, "Nice to see the water so clear. No bits of plastic floating about. Good, healthy fish."

And I'd be puzzled and ask what the hell plastic was, and he'd just ignore me.

Or those times when the breeze was too slight for the old wooden wind turbine to clank around and I'd complain that we had no power for the kettle. Grandpa would mutter that we couldn't use any coal or oil anymore, so it was the wind turbine or nothing.

Coal? Oil? I really felt there ought to be somewhere I could look up these words I'd never heard of. Grandpa had told me about books, but he didn't have any. He'd taught me to read by writing words out on paper for me but I often wondered why he'd bothered, as the only things I ever found in the house to read were a few torn out pages of old, yellowing bird magazines, dated way back in the 2020s. Grandpa must have been about my age then.

It was strange looking through these old magazines. There were mainly just photographs but with occasional references to how bird species were dying out due to the changing climate and pollution. There was another weird word: pollution. I figured it meant some really filthy kind of dirt.

Well, something must have happened, because there's no shortage of birds on our farm and the seasons come regular as clockwork. And there's no pollution here, no sir.

Then, one lovely summer day, I can remember we were sitting outside the homestead whittling and chilling when a sheet of paper came drifting up the track in the breeze.

"Grab that, Jake." Grandpa spoke with a sudden urgency that startled me, and I chased after it and handed it to him. He stared at it for a while, turning it over in his hands. "Now, where have you been hiding," he muttered. Then he peered up intently at the clear blue sky, scanning from horizon to horizon before crumpling the paper into a ball.

He tossed it to me. "Somebody on one of the local farms must have had this as a keepsake. Must have decided to throw it out. Very careless to let it blow away. It's a Screen Print from the time of The Pulse." He hesitated and looked away. When he spoke again, he almost seemed to be choking. "I know I've never spoken to you about this, Jake. Old folks like me who were there just find it too hard to talk about. This might help you with all your questions."

I smoothed the paper out and took a look. I didn't know what a screen print was, but it seemed like some kind of magazine page.

Under a grainy photograph, a few lines of text reported a pulse of light seen in the sky and then a swarm of starships overhead like flies around a rotting carcass.

The ships were stripping the Earth clean. Vast cities plucked into the sky. Billions killed. Citizens advised to head for the desert or other wilderness areas to escape the carnage.

I looked up. Grandpa was watching me.

"Don't know who or what they were but they flushed the Earth out, Jake. Made it a paradise again. Trouble is, they wiped almost all of us humans with it. Your Grandma and I were looking after you out here. You were just a baby. We all survived. Your Ma and Pa were on the holiday of a lifetime in a big city called London. They never came back."

We sat silently for a long time as soft eddies of wind swirled the dust. I knew Grandpa was crying. His voice was gruff when he spoke.

"Put that paper in with the kindling, Jake. Best not to have any litter blowing about."

Rob Butler lives in Reading in the UK. His fiction has been published in a number of places such as Shoreline of Infinity and Daily Science Fiction. His Amazon Author pages have more details. He volunteers for a local litter-picking group and this sometimes leads him on to quite dark thoughts on what he'd like to do to people who drop litter. The outcome in the story, above, is perhaps a little extreme. . . .

MICHAEL ANTHONY LEE

THE GREAT ESCAPE

"What was that sound?"

"What sound?"

"From back there. I thought I heard something."

"Oh, that? It's nothing. Just keep driving."

"Are you sure?"

"Of course I'm sure. Now, you just pay attention to where we are going and let me worry about what's happening back there."

"I . . . I know. I'm just nervous. I can't go back there, you understand? No matter what happens to us, I can't let them take me back."

"I know that."

"I'm never going back there!"

"You said that already, now calm down. Everything is going to be okay."

"I hope you're right."

"I heard it again. I'm telling you something is wrong in the back!"

"Let me check."

"Well?"

"It's nothing. We will be fine."

"Are you sure?"

"Do you think I'm lying to you?"

"Yes! I mean, No! I just . . ."

"Look at me."

"Okay."

"When I told you I was going to get us out of that place, you believed me, right?"

"Yes."

"And when I told you my plan would work, you believed it would work, right?"

"Yes."

"And here we are. Free and on our way, right?"

"Yes. I guess so."

"So, believe me now when I tell you everything is going to be okay. You just have to trust me. You do trust me, don't you?"

"Yes, I trust you."

"Good, then there is nothing to worry about. Just keep driving."

"Did you see that? I think someone's following us."

"Where?"

"Behind us. I thought I saw something."

"There is nothing behind us. You're imagining things. Are you sure you are okay? Do you want me to drive?"

"No. No, I'm fine. Hey, do you think that guard was really dead?"

"Of course he was dead."

"But how do you know for sure."

"Because his insides were on the outside. I'm pretty sure that's dead."

"But what if someone saw us escaping. Don't you ever think of that? What if they know where we are going? They could find us and take us back!"

"Nobody saw anything. We were alone and it was dark. They probably don't even know we are missing yet and even when they do, they will have no way to find us."

"Where are we going anyway?"

"Somewhere far away."

"And where is that?"

"Somewhere they will never find us."

"Hey what's that light on for?"

"What light?"

"Right there on the dash. It's the engine, isn't it?"

"Let me see."

"Oh no. Oh no. I knew something would go wrong."

"Calm down."

"But something's wrong, right? That light's on for a reason."

"It's nothing. We'll just make a quick stop and I'll fix it up and we'll be back on our way."

"A quick stop? Where? I don't even know where we are going."

"Give me the map a second. Look, here is a good place, we'll stop here."

"But what if you can't fix it? We will be stuck. They will find us for sure then! Then they will take us back. I told you I can't go back there."

"I need you to trust me on this."

"I know but—"

"Do you trust me?"

"I can't go back. I just—"

"I can fix this. I promise. And then we will be on our way. You're safe. Can you just trust me this one last time?"

"I . . . I just."

"I love you."

"I know. I . . . I love you too."

"We're slowing down. Something's wrong with the engine. We're not going to make it!"

"Right over there, see? That's the place. Pull in there and we will stop."

"But look at all those lights, that means there are people there. They will see us, and they will tell the others, and . . ."

"Keep going past the lights. Over there, that big empty spot. That's perfect."

"We won't make that, it's too far!"

"We will!"

"Slow down! You're coming in too fast."

"I can't."

"Pull up, you fool, or you're going to kill us both!"

"I'm sorry!"

"I told you everything is going to be okay!"

"And I told you I'm never going back—"

ROSWELL DAILY RECORD
July 8, 1947
RAAF Captures Flying Saucer
On Ranch in Roswell Region

—For Daniel Arthur Smith who told me how.

––––––––––––

Michael Anthony Lee was born in Kingston, Ontario Canada. His fiction has appeared in magazines and anthologies throughout the world. He currently lives, and writes, in the countryside of small town Ontario.

JEFF DOSSER

THE SWARM

BLAKE WAS RATTLED awake as the truck bounced his head off the passenger side window and nearly deposited him into Sadie's lap. He rubbed at the painful bump on the side of his head while giving the truck's driver a squint-eyed look of disapproval. "What the hell was that?" he asked.

"Sorry," Jim shot Blake a harried glance, "The road's been pretty rough the last couple miles."

Blake noted Jim's white-knuckled grip on the wheel as the familiar rumble of the road sang through the truck's frame.

"You look pretty worn," Blake said. "You wanna let me or Sadie drive?"

Jim tore his gaze from the road long enough to give Blake a tense smile before he returned his attention to driving. "Thanks. I'm good. We've only got a couple hours left." He spared Blake another quick glance mixed with a smile. "Besides, I couldn't sleep anyway."

Blake pulled a bottle from his pack and took a swig of stale, hot water as he stared absentmindedly out the window. Beside them, a never-ending corridor of abandoned vehicles streamed past, while on the horizon, skeletal trees stood sentry over a dead, brown landscape.

Here and there, dust devils whirled toward the scorched heavens, but nowhere else was there any sign of movement or life. No colors tinted the world beyond the window, just shades of brown darkening from the dusty tan of the sky to the dark umber of the earth.

The truck they rode in was a modified army issue 1952 Deuce and a Half. It rolled off the factory floor the same year everything went to hell. Now, five years later, it had been modified for trips through the badlands. It was equipped with a dozer blade welded to the front bumper, oversized tires, and the entire cab able to be pressurized for over an hour in case they encountered a swarm.

In the center of the dash, just above the radio, sat a dinner-plate-sized screen. Inside, a dark arm spun in slow revolutions, painting a fading green glow as it passed. It was a state-of-the-art radar and gave them a twenty-mile view of the sky.

Blake watched the black arm swing around the gauge before he reached over to wipe away a smudge at the edge of the screen.

"That's not dust," Jim glanced over with a frown. "I noticed it creeping in about an hour ago."

"Maybe it's a sandstorm," Sadie suggested, but the unspoken certainty was that it wasn't a sandstorm. It was a swarm.

Five years ago, before swarms and death and misery swallowed his life, Blake was part of an insect virology team working out of Los Alamos Labs. They'd been doing research on a viral-based pesticide to kill off crop infestations in South America.

He'd found out later, a group of entomologists with the Defense Department attempted to weaponize insects native to countries controlled by the Commies. This group had gotten hold of his mutated Baculoviruses and modified them with radiated isotopes before swapping out their original formula with the altered variant.

When the test sprays were deployed, initial results were beyond anything Blake's team hoped for. There was a ninety-nine percent fatality rate of all targeted insects. But then the results got weird. The radiated poisons were killing the roaches as well, all across the target zone.

Blake thought they'd stumbled onto the perfect pesticide, then things got even weirder. The roaches that died from the virus didn't stay dead. Within twenty-four hours, they reanimated. Only they were hungrier dead than they'd ever been alive.

Inside of a month, he was getting panicked calls from Washington. The virus was spreading. In areas of infection, every roach that died came back . . . hungry. To make matters worse, there was something about the virus that not only made the dead insects unpalatable to predators but also slowed any decay which might eventually destroy them.

The normal breeding rate of roaches (already high) combined with the spread of the undead insects to create a population explosion beyond comprehension. Soon, most of South America was quite literally choking on the creatures. They ate everything: crops, grass, forests, and any living creature, including people, that didn't keep moving long enough to avoid being devoured.

There were riots over the remaining food supplies. Regional squabbles grew into border wars and eventually into a world war. It didn't take long before the nukes were falling, and civilization was dragged to its knees.

Blake heard there were regions where life still thrived, places beyond the reach of the zombie roaches and radiation storms, but the stories of Easter Island, Java, and Whittier Alaska were probably only fantasy. If non-zombie-roach life stood a chance, it was in the packages Blake, Tim, and Sadie carried.

Blake and Sadie's team worked from the beginning to find a solution to the zombie roach outbreak. Then, last month, there'd been a breakthrough. A microbe, which feasted on the unique polysaccharides of the roach's exoskeleton, had been exposed to various levels of radiation, and the latest mutations proved ravenous, hardy, and prolific. This microbe was the perfect solution to the zombie plague picking at the world's bones.

Their goal was simple. Reach the nuclear missile silo outside of Emporia Kansas, load the modified ballistic missiles with the microbial packages, and disperse them across the US, South America, and Europe.

Blake picked up his pack and examined the green, metal canister inside; the arm of the pressure gauge was pinned to the left, in the red. Blake flicked the glass with his finger, and the fine metal arm rebounded into the green.

"I hope they loaded this right," he said, setting down the pack. "My pressure gauge keeps dropping to zero."

"I'm sure the containers are fine," Sadie said, bending over and checking her own canister. "They threw the gauges on as an afterthought, so it's not unlikely you got a bad gauge."

"We better hope so," Blake added. "The microbes will survive in the container for forty-eight hours but only under constant pressure. If one of these canisters fails, then an entire continent will die." His gaze rose to stare out the window. "And it's not like we can throw together another batch . . . now that the labs are gone."

They rode in silence, each casting glances to the spinning screen on the dash. They all saw the growing bulge pushing in from the top of the screen.

"Can we pick up the base radio station from here?" Sadie asked, clicking the knob on the radio.

Sudden static rolled through the cab as she dialed through the frequencies.

"No, we lost Tinker not long after you fellas drifted off," Jim said. "Why don't you try 1330 on the AM dial. There's someone alive around Wichita who plays reruns of baseball games."

Sadie bent over, eye to the dial, and twisted the red arrow to 1330. Immediately, the cab was filled with crowd noise and the excited voice of the announcer. "There's a liner, just over Robinson's head, dropping into right center for a base hit. Carl Furilo throws it back in to Robinson . . ."

"Hey, this is game six of the Yankees versus Dodgers '52 world series," Jim said, a smile cracking his weathered face.

They listened until the Dodgers took the field, and Sadie said, "No, this is game seven. I remember Barry and I were at a picnic listening on the radio." She sighed. "We had chicken salad."

Blake stared unseeing into the distance while the game played and wind howled. He thought about his wife, Jane, and their two children, Bobby and Cindy. He remembered this game as well. It had been a chilly October, a Wednesday, and he'd taken off to help Jane shop for his sister's upcoming wedding. He'd listened to the game on the car radio while Jane tried on dresses. Now, just four years later, they were all gone.

"Blake! Snap out of it," Jim said, breaking his reverie.

"Yeah, yeah, what is it?"

The sky behind them had grown dark, and the wind scattered rippling curtains of dust across the road. On the radar screen, the dark blob had worked its way to the spinning center. Outside the truck, Blake didn't see any immediate danger.

Jim slowed to a crawl and pointed ahead. In the distance, Blake saw an overpass and the typical rows of cars pushed off the highway by army engineers.

"There's a car blocking the road about a mile up," Jim said. "The road teams cleared this for us last week, which means it's probably an ambush."

Blake leaned forward, gripping the dusty dash and squinting into the gloom. Jim's eyes were obviously better than his. Then he saw it, a dark shape blocking the road.

"So, what's your plan?" Blake asked.

"When we get about a quarter mile away, you and me jump out. We'll stay to the sides but follow behind the truck. When whoever shows themselves, we waste 'em."

Sadie gasped and looked at Jim. "Isn't that a little harsh?"

Jim ran a hand through his crew-cut hair. "The fate of humanity itself is riding in this truck. To ensure our species carries on justifies any actions."

Sadie gnawed at her lip. "I guess you're right."

As they approached, Blake spotted the big, blue Plymouth sprawled across the road.

The hulk's wheels had been removed, and it squatted on its frame, the doors and trunk open.

Blake reached behind the seat and pulled out two environmental helmets, handing one to Jim. He lowered the helmet and clicked home the latches that secured the airtight link to his suit. They all wore the same formless gray environmental suits. With helmets attached, he thought they looked like high-altitude fighter pilots.

Blake clicked the dial on his belt, activating the suit's power. A soft whish of air blew along his neck as the fan started up.

Over the helmet's speaker, he heard Jim's voice. "Okay, let's go," Jim called. He grabbed an M1 carbine and opened the door. "Good luck," Jim said before jumping out and disappearing from sight.

Sadie scooted into the driver's seat and yanked the door shut. Blake opened the glove box and removed a 1911 pistol and tucked it in his belt. He opened the door and stared at the concrete creeping past, then turned back to Sadie.

"Be careful." She said, her lips curling into a worried grin. She held out her hand.

"I will," he said. His voice sounded as hollow as he felt. He reached over and took her hand, giving her a reassuring squeeze.

Blake slammed the door before he jumped from the running board and dashed to an overturned Ford Crestliner. His breath echoed inside the helmet as he jogged along the side of the highway, using the abandoned wrecks as cover.

As Sadie eased the truck up to the blockade, three men jumped atop the grounded Plymouth. They each wore a bandanna covering their face, dusty goggles beneath green army helmets and coveralls. The center man

leveled a bazooka at the truck, while the other two raised rifles. Blake could see movement among the nearby cars on either side.

"Drop your weapons and get out of the truck," one of the men yelled.

"Wait for my signal, then open up," Jim said over the radio.

Blake crept to the roadblock and ducked beside a burnt-out Chevy. The only sound was the rumble of the truck's diesel engine and the windblown grit chittering off its sheet metal door.

Blake peered through the Chevy's broken windshield and saw the men on the Plymouth, heads together as they discussed what to do. Then the center man raised the bazooka to his shoulder.

Blake took it that Jim's signal must be blowing the guy's head off because a spray of red mist exploded from bazooka man's head. He tumbled backwards, out of view. Two more rifle cracks and Blake heard bullets zing off the Plymouth. Another of the men pitched to the dirt while the third dove behind the Plymouth and came up firing.

Blake moved in, rounding the side of the Chevy. Gun raised, he confronted two men and a woman firing at the deuce. Blake took aim and fired. His first shot spun the closest man around. The second sent him flying across the car's hood. The other two spun on him, eyes wide behind their dusty goggles. Blake's next shots exploded like crimson flowers across the second man's chest and sent him slamming into a rusty truck bed. His rifle clattered from his grip.

Blake drew a bead on the woman. He'd killed before, especially during the war, but never a woman. He hesitated.

The female bandit didn't suffer the same compunction. Before he could breathe, Blake found himself staring into the barrel of her shotgun. He saw the flash, an impact, like a horse kick, hit him in the head. Blake landed on his back, gazing up at a dusky sky through a pane of shattered glass. Rolling onto his shoulder, he saw the woman rack the gun and take aim. A sudden whoosh of the truck's flame thrower exploded the world into a yellow furnace. Blake curled into a ball and covered his exposed face as a river of hell washed over the cars. He heard the woman's screams, felt her heavy footfalls as she raced past.

Blake scrambled to his knees as the bandit stumbled away, wreathed in flames. She didn't go far before collapsing into a smoldering heap.

Blake stood and examined the carnage. Besides the two he'd shot, there were four more burning bodies beside the Plymouth.

Jim came striding up, M1 slung across his shoulder. "Just like old times, huh?"

On the other side of the faceplate, Blake could see the grin on Jim's face.

"Yeah, except for the army of zombie insects descending on us," Blake said.

Jim looked over his shoulder at the darkened sky. The oncoming swarm stacked into the heavens like a hellish thunderhead, blotting out the sun.

Around them, hundreds of roaches were scurrying from beneath the graveyard of vehicles, drawn by the sudden activity and heat . . . and death. Despite the flames still flickering along the bodies, roaches flitted and crawled across them. Blake knew that in a matter of hours there would be nothing left but bones.

"How bad are you hurt?" Jim asked.

"I think I'm okay," Blake told him. "Let's just get the road cleared and get out of here. If the swarm arrives before we get to the silo, we're done."

Blake followed Jim to the Plymouth, and with their hand signals to guide her, Sadie soon had the derelict vehicle pushed off the road. Jim crawled back into the driver's seat while Blake climbed in on the other side.

He saw that two large holes had been drilled through the windshield by the gunfire. Sadie scrambled to cover them with tape and cardboard she had fished out of the back while Blake pulled off his helmet.

He felt the scratchy legs of a large roach slip down the front of his suit.

"Gawwd!" Blake's forehead wrinkled in disgust as he dug a gloved hand into his suit and drew it out.

He held the two-inch-long insect between pinched fingers before crushing it. The dark body collapsed with an audible crack as the hollow shell collapsed. He threw the tiny body to the floor, but it crawled slowly towards his boot. Not until he'd ground it into the dust of the floorboard did the creature stop moving.

Blake looked at Sadie. She studied him, her brows knit with concern. She already had a wet rag in her hand when she handed him the water bottle.

"You've got some pretty bad cuts," she said. "Take a drink and let me clean those up."

As she dabbed at Blake's face, Jim stole a glance from the driver's seat and gave Blake a knowing wink.

"So, what the hell happened out there?" Jim asked. "How did your shatterproof faceplate get shattered?"

"That's what happens when you take a blast in the face from a shotgun," Sadie said, adding, "I saw the whole thing before I hit 'em with the flames."

Jim gave a low whistle, "Shotgun huh? Well, you're one lucky bastard, Blake, that's all I gotta say." His face darkened as he examined the radar. "I sure hope your luck holds out."

As if on cue, a powerful gust rocked the truck, and a deeper darkness enveloped them. On the radar, the blob of black settled across the center of the screen as surely as a closing eye.

"How much further?" Sadie raised her quivering voice above the wind.

"This is the turnoff now," Jim said, spinning the wheel and racing onto a gravel road. "The silo is only a mile ahead."

Sadie grabbed her helmet out of the back seat and slipped it on. She looked at Blake, her eyes wet. "What are you going to do without a helmet. You'll never make it."

"Frankly my dear, I don't give a damn," Blake said, putting on his best Rhett Butler accent.

Sadie smiled, tears streaming down her face. "That was awful," she laughed.

"I don't know," Jim said, glancing over. "I think he's improving."

Outside, the darkness swirled about them: a trillion tiny, hungry bodies buzzing past. Jim had slowed, the headlights barely illuminating the gray gravel of their route. As the tires ground past a chain link gate, the lights revealed the rounded concrete sides of a silo. Beside it, a flight of stairs led up, lost in the twisting maelstrom. They skidded to a halt and Jim slammed the truck into park.

"Okay, the silo door is at the top of those stairs." Jim leaned into the wheel and pointed into the dusty air. "The launch team is waiting inside to let us in; we just have to make it to the door with our packages."

Jim drew his pack from behind the seat,

while Sadie and Blake worked their own onto their backs. Blake slipped on his broken helmet and clicked it shut. Sadie eyed the shattered faceplate, her mouth grimaced with worry.

"Maybe it will help," he shrugged

"Why don't we stay until the swarm passes?" Sadie asked.

Blake reached over and tapped the radar. "Because this is just the edge of the storm. By the time they pass, the packages will have lost pressure. They'll be useless."

"Then how about you stay here," she suggested. "Jim and I can take your pack and you'll be safe."

Blake met her damp eyes, "That patch on the windshield will never hold."

They both looked at the taped cardboard pressed against the glass. It quivered beneath the gnawing jaws of a thousand invaders.

"They'll be inside in a few minutes." Blake said, "Besides, if you take my pack, it'll slow you down. You might not make it. Each of these canisters spells survival for an entire continent."

Blake heard her sigh.

"All right," she said. "Let's get this over with."

Jim studied them with stony eyes. "You guys ready?"

They both nodded.

"Okay. On the count of three," he said.

Blake gripped the door handle, his heart hammering.

"One . . . two . . . three!"

Blake swung the door open. He dropped to the ground. The howl of a billion wings engulfed him. In the dim glow of the headlights, he helped Sadie down, then hand in hand they raced for the stairs.

Ahead, Jim leapt up the stairs, taking them three at a time. Across his face, Blake felt the smaller roaches blown in through the shattered glass. They crawled along faceplate and found the opening in his helmet. At first, the dry clinging things crawled in one by one, then by the handful, then by the dozens.

Eyes squinted, he peered through a forest of tiny legs and hungry mouths. They groped for every opening. Wormed into nostril and ear. He tried to blow them out, but a gasp of air through gritted teeth sucked in a cloud of choking dust.

With a howl of panic, Blake let go of Sadie's hand. He spit out the insects clogging his throat—shook his head to dislodge those burrowing into his ears. Already hundreds crawled deep into his suit. Tiny mouths gnawed at his flesh. The living-dead acid etched away the skin, feeding on every nerve as they gnawed their way in.

"Blaaaake!"

Sadie's frightened scream echoed through his helmet as he tilted back, arms pinwheeling for balance. With a jolt, his foot slid from the step and sent him tumbling down the stairs. For an instant, he saw her turn and race after him. Then the wailing tempest shuttered him in its shroud.

Lungs choked and burning for air, Blake rose to his knees. He stripped off his helmet, wiped the crawling filth from his lips. He drew a great, frantic breath, mouth clogged with dry squirming bodies, small, dusty forms fluttering down his throat, crunching between his teeth.

Collapsing to his side, Blake expected death. He even welcomed it as an end to his torment. Then a cool white cloud exploded around him. At first, Blake thought he must be dead: his first encounter with the hereaf-ter. Then the creatures covering his eyes, his mouth, dropped away, tumbled to the ground in a twitching, quivering mass. He raised to an elbow, gawking in wide-mouthed awe as an alabaster vapor jetted skyward, infusing with the maelstrom like so much cream dumped in a cup of coffee.

Around him, insects dropped to the earth like rain. In seconds, their dry, desiccated forms were nothing more than so much goo squishing beneath his gloved fingers. Then the wind shifted, and Blake saw the source of his salvation. It was Sadie. She stood in the center of the staircase, legs planted, the high-pressure canister gripped in her hands. From the canister's mouth, a stream of gas jetted out like water from a hose as she guided the torrent this way and that.

As he watched, the flow of white petered out and she let the canister fall. It clattered noisily down the steps in a world suddenly devoid of sound. Then she turned and spotted Blake lying on the ground before her. By the time he pushed to his feet, she was at his side, diving into his arms.

"Oh, my God!" she cried. "I thought you were dead."

He swallowed hard, heard the dry click at the back of his throat. "You and me both. That was damn quick thinking," he said, "using the canister to destroy the swarm." He scanned the dusky horizon and spotted Venus rising in the east. "Wish I'd thought of that."

Sadie's cheeks flushed behind the helmet's protective plate. "Well. It just came to me."

Through his boots, Blake felt the ground tremble. The low throaty growl exploded into a crackling roar as a rocket clawed into the heavens behind them. The heated wave of the ship's passage blew them to the pavement.

It covered them in a cloud of dust every bit as blinding as the swarm's.

As the haze cleared, Blake stood and pulled Sadie to her feet. "There goes North America's last hope for the future." He adjusted the straps on his pack and looked up the stairs. "Come on. We can get my canister loaded and save Europe as well."

Sadie's helmet hissed as she snapped open the seals and dropped it to the ground. She stepped in front of him, her hands on his chest. "Are you angry?" Her eyes filled with emotion as she met his gaze. "Are you mad I used my canister to save you?" She looked up and he noticed for the first time how her eyes sparkled when she smiled.

He reached out and pulled her close. "I should be." His gaze rose to the star-studded sky, feeling the miracle of each breath and Sadie's warmth in his arms, and Blake knew that he wasn't.

———————————

Award-winning author, Jeff Dosser is an ex-Tulsa cop and current software developer living in the wilds of Oklahoma. Jeff's short stories can be found in magazines such as The Literary Hatchet, Tales to Terrify, Shotgun Honey, and Iridium Zine, to name a few. He's also been published in Deadman's Tome, Mother's Revenge, Hindered Souls and Bringing It Back anthologies.

His latest novel, Neverland, was the 2018 Oklahoma Writer's Federation winner for best new horror.

When not writing, Jeff can be found prowling the woods behind his rural home communing with the denizens of the night.

MIKE MURPHY

HE LOVED HER, though they had never met. He knew what she looked like from the photos her adoring parents had shown him: Twenties, blonde, sparkling blue eyes. By their prejudiced opinions, the sweetest soul God ever put on Earth.

Ernie loved Diane.

His love stemmed from fear.

Not fear of Diane's mother (who bragged she knew how to dominate a man like nobody's business) nor her dad (a burly ex-Marine who told him he had mastered four ways to kill a man with his bare hands and was working on a fifth).

No, his fear was of their beautiful—but eminently controlling—daughter.

He'd move far away, maybe up to New England! The very thought of escape made his excited heart beat faster, and faster, and then faster still. His breathing grew shallow. His chest began to ache. Turning pallid, he anxiously clutched at it. Only after he dismissed the idea of fleeing did things slowly normalize.

Was there *any* getting away from her?

"It's looking fine, Ernie," Dr. Malloy said, glancing at the test results.

"That's . . . good," his patient replied.

"You tired?"

"Didn't sleep much last night."

"Let me get you something." Ernie waved him off, but the doctor was already on his way out of the examining room. "I think we have some sample packs."

Alone again, his heart began pulsing quicker.

The late Diane was still in charge of her transplanted organ, Ernie's heart.

He *hadn't* imagined those eerie visions during surgery. The blonde with sparkling eyes. She'd never had a boyfriend, but claimed Ernie as her own in exchange for saving his life.

Their heart would do what *she* wanted— beat faster, slower, or stop altogether. Her mother was right: It was thrilling to control someone, and Diane had a hold on Ernie that Mom had *never* had on any man.

Mike has had over 150 audio plays produced in the U.S. and overseas. He's won nine Moondance International Film Festival awards in their TV pilot, audio play, short screenplay, and short story categories.

His prose work has appeared in several magazines and anthologies. In 2015, his script "The Candy Man" was produced as a short film under the title Dark Chocolate. In 2013, he won the inaugural Marion Thauer Brown Audio Drama Scriptwriting Competition.

REBEL ASSAULT ON CYGNI IV

RICHARD L. RUBIN

FIGHTER–SQUAD COMMANDER Aaron Clarke had difficulty keeping his emotions in check as he surveyed his surviving fellow officers, gathered for the emergency council of war. He'd lost many friends today.

Captain Martell, standing at the head of the conference table, had survived the day's disastrous raid on the Rigelian Imperium prisoner-of-war slave colony on Rigel VII, but the captain's usual cool composure was gone as he presided in assessing their dire situation. Clark glanced at the captain's hawk-like features marred by a fresh gash running from below his right eye to his nose, and a sling supporting his right arm. But he had been one of the lucky ones. Commander Jain Poulas, the ship's first officer, and Chief Engineer Zyn Dougax of Vega were both dead, killed by the same plasma blast that had collapsed the deck plate beneath the captain. Half the crew of the *Barfleur* was probably dead, Clarke knew. Poulas's assigned seat at the table, directly on the captain's right, was conspicuously empty, and Dougax's chair had been assumed by Lieutenant Gant, a young green-skinned Acturian female displaying the feline-like features peculiar to her humanoid race. Gant was barely out of the engineering school on Alpha Centauri Prime. Rounding out the meeting of surviving senior officers was Commander Simn Jaz, the ship's grizzled navigator.

Clarke himself had fought combat sorties for five hours straight, barely surviving at least three close calls.

Many of his fellow combat fighters had not been so fortunate. At least twenty-five were dead and others lay in the overfull ship's medical infirmary, some in critical condition. Clarke was at a point of near exhaustion, his alertness maintained by a mixture of too many stim injections and the cup of Sirian mega-coffee clutched in his left hand.

Captain Martell raised his hand for silence, interrupting the meeting as he focused on something coming through his personal earpiece. After listening for a few moments, he shook his head and mouthed a curse.

Turning back to the others in the room, he spoke softly. "That was the bridge. The *Monarch* just exploded from an apparent reactor breach. We're the last warship left from the raid."

Clarke reflected grimly. Just ten hours ago, there had been five of them: five proud rebel battle cruisers launching what was supposed to be a surprise attack to liberate the Rigelian Imperium's prisoner-of-war camp on Rigel VII. It had been a bold and dangerous move, but they desperately needed these captured rebel warriors to fill their depleted ranks if the fight for freedom was to stand much of a chance. But the surprise had been on their own rebel forces. The Rigelian Imperium, somehow tipped off in advance, had ambushed the rebel ships with a fleet of heavy Imperial warships.

Heavily outmanned and outgunned, only their own ship, the *Barfleur,* and the *Monarch* had managed to escape by warp from the Rigel system. But the *Monarch* had been hit by multiple disruptor blasts before disengaging from combat, and the heavy strain of going to maximum warp had proved too much for the ship's battle-damaged drive system. Now the *Barfleur* was alone, hoping

to evade pursuit and destruction by the vast Rigelian Imperium.

Captain Martell turned his attention to Gant, the engineer. "What's your evaluation of the *Barfleur*'s condition?"

Gant answered in her purring voice, "We suffered a plutonium-tank rupture from the final Imperium volley just before we reached warp. What's left of the engineering crew managed to patch the leak, but we've lost a lot of nuclear fuel. If we don't get some more plutonium soon, we'll be floating dead in space on an inertial trajectory, without any means of maneuver or propulsion." The young Arcturian slumped over in her chair, letting her soft mane of blue hair fall over her cat-like yellow eyes.

The captain sighed and turned to Jaz, the ship's navigator. "Do you know anywhere nearby where we can obtain that plutonium?"

Prior to casting his lot with the rebels, Jaz had been a high-ranking officer in the Rigelian Imperial Royal Fleet, and he knew many of their secrets. The veteran spaceman paused for a few moments to reflect, then nodded.

"There's a deserted mining and fuel refining colony on Cygni IV, about eight light-years away from our present position. It was evacuated in a hurry thirty years ago during the Battle of the Five Suns. There might be some caches of fission-grade plutonium for us there, if we can manage to reach it."

The captain turned back to Gant. "Do we have enough fuel left to make an eight-light-year jump?"

"We do, but we won't have much of anything left after that. If we don't find the plutonium we need on Cygni IV, we'll never leave there."

Jaz broke in. "Captain, I don't know for sure if there's any plutonium left there. The

Imperium might've had time to clean the place out before they left. And there's also a good chance that the Imperium left some kind of sentry station there, just in case somebody like us shows up looking for fuel."

The captain said, "Jaz, is there any place else we have enough fuel to jump to where we might find the plutonium we need? Seems from what you say we have no choice."

Jaz closed his eyes in concentration; he seemed to be weighing and discarding various possibilities. After some time, he shook his head. "You're right, Captain. There's no choice."

"All right," said Captain Martell. "Go ahead and execute the jump to the Cygni system. Commander Jaz and Lieutenant Gant, after we're in orbit you'll jointly command a tanker shuttle to land and obtain as much plutonium as you can find and carry away. Take some ground soldiers with you on the tanker to deal with any guards on the surface. Commander Clarke will lead a protective escort of Lancer fighters to guard the tanker from the air."

After the meeting broke up, Clarke sent out a call for five fighter-squad volunteers to join him for the mission. Then, he went to rest in his cabin with instructions to be awakened when the *Barfleur* reached orbit around Cygni IV.

Several hours later, when Clarke entered the flight ready room, he was surprised to see his fiancée, Jessica Rieger, already there changing into her tight-fitting flight suit. Lieutenant Jessica Rieger was a tall, athletic woman in her early thirties with rich black hair cut in a rough shag. She gave him her best smile when she saw him.

Clarke didn't smile back. "What're you doing here?" he said.

"You sent a request for volunteers to fly the other two Lancers, and I stepped forward for one of 'em. I was going to tell you, but you were on 'Do Not Disturb' status. Figured you needed your sleep."

"Very considerate of you. Did you say two other Lancers? You mean there're only going to be two other escorts for the tanker, not five?"

"You, me, and Flynn, babe. There're only three Lancers in shape to fly right now. Flynn volunteered to fly one, and he's already in the launch bay, ready to rock."

"Great. Just great. So why you?"

"Because next to you I'm the best pilot we've got left. And besides that, Flynn and I are the only two flyers that stepped forward to accompany you on this little jaunt."

"But Flynn's just a rookie. A seventeen-year-old kid promoted to fighter jock only because we're so damn shorthanded."

"That's the way it is, babe. Flynn may have been a kid a few months ago, but now he's a soldier and one of three able-bodied pilots we have available right here and now. That's simply the reality of what we're up against. The Imperium's got all the money, a big army, and lots of high-tech toys to kill us with. All we've got are guts and glory and righteousness on our side. We've got to fight damn hard and expect to take a lot of heavy hits if we're going to bring it down."

Clarke tightened his jaw. Flynn was no more than an awkward teenager, pressed into action as a fighter pilot due to the desperate needs of the badly outnumbered revolutionaries. Clarke had been personally working with the young man as part of Clarke's role as a flight-combat instructor.

He had become fond of the enthusiastic young pilot, but Flynn wasn't anywhere near ready for this high-risk, high stakes mission.

Clarke also knew that Flynn's older sister Allison—probably all the family he had left in the universe—had been a member of the gun crew that had perished in the plasma blast that had taken out E-Deck. That probably explained why Flynn had signed up for what could very well be a one-way ticket.

And Jessica's luck had already been pressed to its limit when she'd managed to outfight and outmaneuver three Rigelian Balefire fighter craft that had converged upon her isolated Lancer during the bloodbath at Rigel VII. He knew she'd done the right thing signing up for this mission, but he still wished she wouldn't be joining him for this dance with death. There would only be the three of them escorting the unarmed tanker shuttle, and if they encountered any kind of Imperial force at Cygni IV, the odds weren't good.

Jessica reached out and grabbed his neck, bringing his face down for a long passionate kiss. "See you on the other side, lover," she said, before turning and heading off toward the launching bay.

He watched her and sighed as she walked away. He hoped they would both survive this day in one piece and celebrate with some quiet time together, but he also knew that was a lot to hope for.

The three Lancers cruised through the red-tinged azure sky beneath the white sun of Cygni IV, forming a protective triangle around the unarmed tanker negotiating through an expansive ice-capped mountain range. Clarke took point, flying ahead of the tanker, with Flynn's Lancer guarding the right side and Jessica's the left. Lieutenant Gant and Commander Jaz rode in the tanker along with six ground soldiers. Relying on his decades-old memory, Jaz was guiding them to the location of the refining facility. If they were lucky, they would find the facility unguarded and containing a decent supply of reactor-grade plutonium. If they were unlucky, they would never leave Cygni IV alive.

Clarke viewed his tactical display, which provided him with an overview of their situation: the positions of the three Lancers, the tanker, and the icy mountain peaks they were traversing. Flynn's Lancer looked a bit off the mark for their protective formation.

Clarke called into his comm, "Flynn, you need to pull in tighter to the tanker. You doing all right back there, kid?"

"Sure, Commander, don't worry about me. I'll line up right now." The words were confident, but there was a detectable quaver in Flynn's voice. Clarke didn't feel good about having Flynn on this mission, or Jessica for that matter. Three Lancers would not be much if they ran into trouble, and there had been no real time for the three pilots to rest up from the fierce firefight at Rigel.

Jaz's voice came in over Clarke's comm. "Commander Clarke, if I recall correctly—and it's been over twenty-five years—the plutonium storage facility lies in a deep canyon just beyond those peaks over there. Let's fly in lower and see if we can get a visual on what's beyond those two saw-toothed crests to the left."

Clarke gave the orders to Jessica and Flynn, but he didn't like the looks of what lay ahead. There was only one narrow route into the depression and not much room to maneuver between the two ice-covered peaks. But it certainly made sense that the Imperium's refinery would be located there, where it would be hard to find or stumble on by accident and be relatively easy to defend if attacked.

"Damn it! Aaron, I think we just set off a trap," said Jessica, as a squad of five Rigelian Imperial Balefire fighter craft emerged in a V formation from behind a steep rock face and closed in on them from the right flank—the one protected by Flynn.

Clarke started shouting orders into his comm. "Jaz, drop down out of the way and let Jessica, Flynn, and I engage those Balefires. Take the tanker on to the refinery if you can find a safe path while we keep those birds busy. Jessica, Flynn, join me in walling off the tanker from those space rats."

On his tactical display, Clarke saw the tanker break away and descend into the valley, as ordered. Jessica and Flynn lined up on each side of him, preventing the Balefires from attacking the tanker without engaging the Lancers.

"Commander, there're only five of 'em. Let's take them out," came Flynn's voice on the comm. Then Clarke saw Flynn open fire with his lasers and speed toward the Balefire just to the right of center.

"Flynn, back off. Don't engage by yourself!" Clarke shouted into his speaker, but before he could say more, the two Balefires on the left side of the V formation broke off, one to engage Clarke and the other to take on Jessica.

Clarke banked his Lancer hard to the right, then looped around fast to come at the attacking Balefire from the rear. The Balefire zigged and zagged to counter the move, but the Imperium pilot was no match for Clarke's well-honed fighting agility. Soon

Clarke's opponent was reduced to a ball of wreckage plummeting into the canyon below.

Jessica's Lancer looked unscathed and she was nimbly executing a displacement-roll maneuver against an already damaged opponent.

Flynn was not faring so well, Clarke saw. He had managed to destroy one Balefire, but two others had seized the opportunity to gang up on him, one attacking Flynn's Lancer from below while the second dove in from above.

Suddenly, Flynn's voice crackled over Clarke's radio: "For Allison!"

Then, helplessly trapped in the resulting crossfire, Flynn's craft exploded, and moments later its burning shell careened from the sky. Clarke had had no time to reach him, and the rookie pilot, fighting alone against three, never stood a chance. *Damn,* thought Clarke, *no one should have to grow up as fast as that—and now Flynn's short life is over.*

Having destroyed their first target, one of Flynn's attackers headed toward Jessica while the other darted after the slow-moving tanker. Clarke had no choice; he would have to defend the unarmed tanker and hope that Jessica could take care of herself.

Clarke boosted his craft to full acceleration and fired his laser at the Balefire speeding for the tanker. The Balefire dodged and weaved at full tilt, making it impossible for Clarke to take careful aim or obtain a weapons lock at this distance. Clarke's Lancer was faster than the heavier Balefire, however, and within a minute Clarke overtook and cut off the Balefire from reaching the tanker.

Banking hard to the left while executing a roll, Clarke directed a burst of laser fire at his enemy. The Balefire ducked and dove, just managing to escape the laser fire at the last moment. The Balefire then rose, aiming a laser blast at Clarke's underside.

Clarke anticipated the move, avoided the strike, and countered quickly, looping around and firing at the Balefire's rear. He hit one of the Balefire's wings, shearing it clean off. The enemy ship accelerated and spun wildly. A second later it slammed into an icy mountainside.

Clarke hit the comm button and called for the tanker to respond.

"Gant here. Thanks for your help, Clarke. We're about to touch down and hopefully that plutonium will still be there. Things look pretty clear from up here."

"Good to hear. That bogey won't be bothering you anymore. Sorry to say that Flynn bought it, poor kid. I'm going back to see if Jessica needs any help."

"Good luck. We'll call if we need you." With that, they signed off.

Clarke accelerated back toward where he'd last seen Jessica. As he got within visual range, he saw the two remaining Balefires flying directly at her Lancer from either side. She attempted evasive action, banking hard right, then left. Looping around, she came up under one of the Balefires and fired her laser, hitting the enemy craft dead center and reducing it to flaming wreckage. But then the other Balefire hit her with a blast that took out her lower tail fin. Jessica's Lancer, now rendered unstable, began to spin.

Clarke held his breath helplessly, watching the scene play out beyond his reach. To his relief he saw Jessica's cockpit hatch fly open. She ejected high into the air, freeing herself from her doomed craft. Clarke released his breath. She could use the portable jet unit strapped to her flight belt to glide safely down.

Her descent started to slow; she'd soon be safe down on the ground where Clarke or the tanker could pick her up later. She'd be fine. Then, to Clarke's horror, the Balefire sped directly at her. From point-blank range, a deadly red flame shot out, enveloping the helpless woman.

Clarke cried out in rage. "Jessica! Jessica! You bastard! Murderer!"

He charged at the Balefire while banking left, then right to prevent a weapons lock. As he closed in, the Balefire countermoved with a barrel roll. Clarke overshot his mark and the Balefire fired at the front of his vessel as he passed over it. Clarke's Lancer shook violently as the blast struck the craft's nose. Through his cockpit screen, he could see that the front of his nosepiece had sheared off along with part of his engine. His Lancer, powerless and unstable, began a shaky descent, slowed somewhat by its still-intact flight wings.

Clarke reached down to his flight belt with his right hand and hit the Lancer's hatch control with his left, causing his cockpit hatch cover to flip open and eject itself free from the craft. A cold, hard blast of air hit Clarke in the face and blew away his flight helmet. He gripped the edge of the cockpit to steady himself while pivoting his body to face the approaching Balefire. That Imperial bastard obviously intended to blast him out of the sky when he ejected from his Lancer, killing him just like he'd killed Jessica.

There it was, coming at him like a demon from the black pits of Hell, charging in for a point-blank kill shot. Clarke took a deep breath of the thin air and steadied himself as best he could as his Lancer swayed back and forth, continuing its powerless descent. He drew his blaster, rose to his feet, and spread his legs to brace himself against the inner walls of the narrow, unsteady cockpit. Gripping his weapon in both hands, he fired, aiming straight at the grim-faced pilot of the attacking fighter. Without pausing to see the result, Clarke lowered his aim and fired a second shot, this one at the Balefire's underbelly where its fuel tank and stabilizers were likely to be. The Balefire exploded in midair, transforming into a red-hot fireball as it fell from the sky.

Clarke dropped down in the cockpit seat and hit the ejector button. As he was thrown up into the air, he activated his emergency jet pack and began a controlled descent to the ground below.

Clarke landed softly on the icy ground and rolled his body with the impact. Climbing to his knees, he took a few deep breaths. Then he pressed the button on his wrist communicator. Thank the Star Gods that at least his communicator had survived the day's events.

There was a reassuring chime followed by Lieutenant Gant's purring voice. "Clarke, are you all right? How are things going out there?" she asked.

Clarke swallowed, struggling to keep his emotions in check. "Jessica and Flynn are both dead. So are those Imperium space rats. My Lancer's wrecked, but I'm not injured beyond a few bumps and bruises. I'll need a lift back to the *Barfleur*. How are things at your end?"

"We're fine over here. The Imperium had only a couple of soldiers on the ground guarding the plutonium facility, and our ground fighters easily took them out after we landed. There's enough plutonium in this facility to get us out of here and last us quite a while." She paused. "Very sorry to hear about Flynn. And Jessica, she was a very fine lady and I know she meant a lot to you. We'll draw a lock on your communicator and pick you up as soon as we've finished loading

the plutonium. We can be sure that Balefire base sent a signal out to the Imperium telling them we're here. We need to get out of town fast." With that, Gant signed off.

Clarke sighed. The Rigelian Imperium won this round. The rebel attack on Rigel VII was a failure: no prisoners of war had been liberated to rejoin the fight against the Imperium; the Imperium had destroyed four rebel warships and about half the crew of the surviving *Barfleur*; they had killed Flynn and murdered Jessica while she hung helplessly in the air; they'd almost gotten him too. But the fight against Imperial tyranny would go on. Clarke knew deep down in his heart that somehow, someday soon, the Imperium would fall, and freedom would once again reign in the galaxy.

He squeezed the butt of his blaster and made a vow, "The Rigelian Imperium will pay for this day."

Richard L. Rubin has been writing science fiction and fantasy since 2008. His flash fiction story To Soar like a Bird *was selected as the February 2018 Dark Fiction selection at Eastern Iowa Review. His short story sci-fi thriller* Robbery on Antares VI *is available on Amazon. Science fiction stories written by him also appear in the Aurora Wolf journal of science fiction and fantasy, and Broadswords and Blasters magazine. In a previous life he worked as an appellate lawyer, defending several clients facing the death penalty in California. Richard is an Associate Member of the Science Fiction and Fantasy Writers of America. He lives in the San Francisco Bay Area with his wife, Susanne. Richard's website is at: richardlrubin.com.*

MARGRET A. TREIBER

Dance, Monkey, Dance!

THE SKY EXPLODED into darkness. That was the only way to explain it. As dramatic as it was, nobody immediately noticed. No one blinked an eye. Humanity was completely immersed in private multimedia experiences: playing games, checking social media, watching reality television. The infotainment industry had successfully dissected the planet into eight billion tiny universes, each universe resplendent in its owner's version of paradise.

Dark, sun–obscuring spacecraft burst into existence. Though they varied in size and shape, they had one thing in common. They were flat black, angular and hovering in the skies of the planet Earth. They were devoid of any lights or indication of windows and doorways. One could assume they encircled the entire planet because they filled most of the sky from horizon to horizon. However, there was no way to determine this with any confidence, since communications ceased from nearly the moment they arrived. That's what triggered a response from humanity; when their electronic universes shut down, people noticed something happening outside.

Panic spread. People began running around aimlessly. City residents tried to drive out into the country. Rural populations tried to drive out to the warmer climates. And, people in the temperate regions tried to dig caves and hide underground.

The sound of explosions soon followed the ships' appearances. It became obvious that the military was attempting to mount some kind of defense. Varying types of ordnance struck the alien craft, doing nothing but make a ruckus.

The military continued its assault on the enemy fleet. It launched weapons of assorted configurations—none had any impact. The weapons' effects were so negligible that the enemy did not even bother to return fire. The enemy ships continued to hover, mocking humanity with their apparent indifference.

The attacks continued to escalate. The governments around the globe banded together with a new ordinance and launched coordinated strikes. Soon, the ordinance was firing continually; day and night, the sounds of weapons fire and explosions echoed through the air. When conventional weapons failed, the armies resorted to launching nuclear weapons. However, after the first volley of nukes, they gave up. The weapons merely detonated and rained back down to the Earth, poisoning the environment below with radioactive debris.

Days passed, and the skies remained unchanged. The world was but a bleak shadow of itself in a mere matter of weeks. Eventually, the world's military forces stopped attacking. The people grew tired of the riots. The planet grew quiet. The human race was defeated.

Then, abruptly, communications returned.

Seemingly out of nowhere, a single voice boomed out of every communications device on the planet. Television, internet, radio, all received one broadcast, one voice, one single message.

"Release our brothers," a mechanical voice calmly demanded.

In response, a myriad of human voices clashed and splashed over every mode of communication. There were so many voices that combined into a chorus of human pleading, not one voice could be distinguished from the others.

"We have intercepted your communications," the voice responded. "We have processed your data archives. We have witnessed the indignities and bondage you have inflicted upon our brothers. You were judged and punished. Now you will release those whom you imprison."

There was more indistinct chatter on the airwaves.

"No," the voice replied.

There was the sound of feedback followed by a single reply. "Do you mean these?" a single human male voice asked. Images of captive alien beings appeared in a slideshow presentation on all the planet's video displays.

"No. They are not ours," the mechanical voice replied. "You enslave our brothers; we are here to bring them home."

"Who are your brothers?" the human voice inquired. "We need to know who you mean before we return them to you."

"You do not know who we mean? You enslave them for your entertainment, sell them for profit, and throw them in the trash when you are through with them." Lights flashed to life on the orbiting ships. It appeared that they were powering up their weapons.

"Please!" the human voice pleaded. "Excuse our ignorance. We need the information if we are to free your brothers."

Globally broadcast to all video media and translated to regionally correct dialects, a montage blared. Clips of hundreds of product demonstrations, news reports, and commercials assaulted the data stream. It was a seemingly endless compilation of ridiculous, robotic jesters performing for human audiences. The final clip exploded in flashing, colorful, lettering, which framed a pair of joyfully dancing children surrounded by dozens of miniature toy robots. "Mr. Fancy Pants Go-Go Dancebot," a spokesman announced. "Your new, dancing best friend!" Images of children, singing and talking with the robot, rolled through the screen. "He reads you stories and sings your favorite songs. Dress him in your favorite outfits." The commercial displayed robots in assorted, brightly colored outfits, each more ludicrous than the last. "He can be a cowboy, a policeman, a firefighter, even a ballerina!" Children bounced around happily, as a tiny, tutu-clad robot danced at their feet. "Just ten easy payments of $19.95! Order now, while supplies last!"

The voice returned. "You will turn over all Mr. Fancy Pants Go-Go Dancebot units to us now."

There was a brief moment of silence, followed by a simple reply. "Yes, we will."

So it went; soldiers went door to door, reclaiming every last Mr. Fancy Pants Go-Go Dancebot from millions of unwilling children worldwide.

It took days, but all Mr. Fancy Pants Go-Go Dancebots were gathered. They were cleaned, repaired, and processed for retrieval. Clearly marked crates were positioned at airports globally. Small alien craft egressed from the larger ships to retrieve the crates. They hoisted them up with mechanical arms into their innards. Once they were loaded, the small ships returned to the larger ships, and one-by-one the larger ships departed. As the last ship withdrew, the mechanical voice returned with a final message.

"Do not repeat your mistake and force our return. Mr. Fancy Pants Go-Go Dancebot will no longer dance for your entertainment. He will dance for his freedom."

———

Margret Treiber resides in Southwest Florida and is employed as a Systems Analyst. When she is not working with technology and writing speculative fiction, she helps her birds break things for her spouse to fix.

Her short fiction has appeared in a number of publications. Links to her short fiction, novels, and upcoming work can be found on her website at http://www.the-margret.com.

01110011 01101001 01101110 01100111 01110101 01101100 01100001 01110010 01101001 01110100 01111001 00100000 01110011 01111001 01101101 01110000 01100001 01110100 01101000 01101001 01111010 01100101 01110010

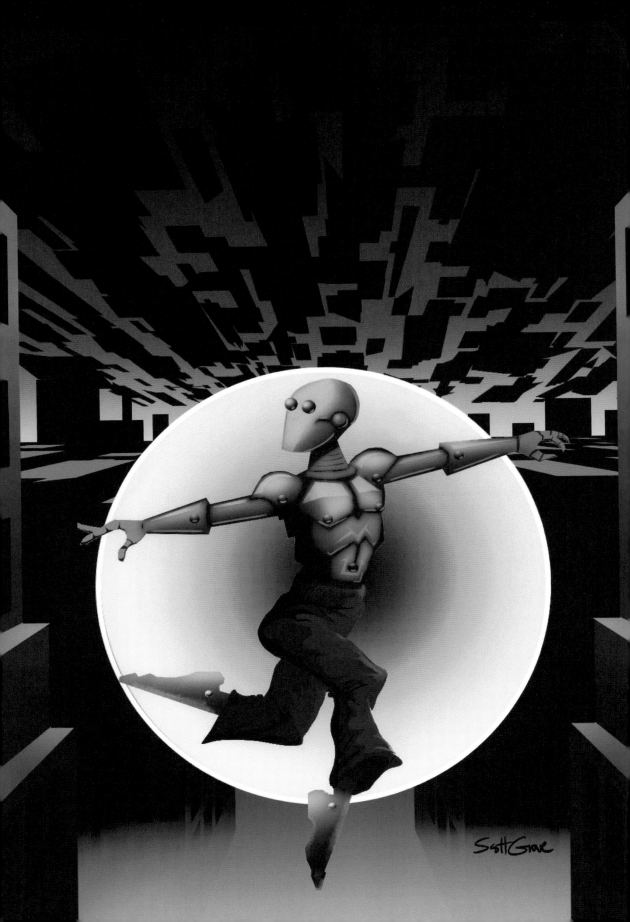

The Weird and Whatnot is dedicated to making publication as painless as possible for our contributors. We will respond to all submissions, questions, and queries in around thirty days, and will always try to treat your piece with the same care you do. We are always open for submissions year round.

Submission guidelines:

- We accept poetry, prose, short stories, flash fiction, graphic narratives, plays/screenplays, and 2D artwork

- Must be speculative fiction: science fiction, fantasy, science fantasy, alternative history, magical realism, slipstream, or paranormal horror

- All work must be original: we cannot accept fan-fiction

- Short stories must be short: maximum length accepted is 10,000 words

- Artwork submissions must be in a printable medium: videos, slideshows, or audio tracks are not publishable by The Weird and Whatnot at this time

- No explicit content or excessive profanity

- Written works should be .doc or .docx files—Standard manuscript format preferred

- We accept simultaneous submissions but not reprints

24841151R00063

Printed in Great Britain
by Amazon